# Samuel Rutherford

---

*Alexander Whyte*

# Contents

I. JOSHUA REDIVIVUS ............................................................7

II. SAMUEL RUTHERFORD AND SOME OF HIS EXTREMES ....... 13

III. MARION M'NAUGHT ................................................... 19

IV. LADY KENMURE ....................................................... 25

V. LADY CARDONESS .................................................... 29

VI. LADY CULROSS ....................................................... 34

VII. LADY BOYD ........................................................... 39

VIII. LADY ROBERTLAND .............................................. 45

IX. JEAN BROWN .......................................................... 52

X. JOHN GORDON OF CARDONESS, THE YOUNGER ..............59

XI. ALEXANDER GORDON OF EARLSTON ......................... 64

XII. EARLSTON THE YOUNGER ....................................... 70

XIII. ROBERT GORDON OF KNOCKBREX .......................... 76

XIV. JOHN GORDON OF RUSCO ..................................... 82

XV. BAILIE JOHN KENNEDY ........................................... 89

XVI. JAMES GUTHRIE ................................................... 94

XVII. WILLIAM GUTHRIE ............................................. 101

XVIII. GEORGE GILLESPIE ........................................... 107

XIX. JOHN FERGUSHILL ............................................... 114

XX. JAMES BAUTIE, STUDENT OF DIVINITY ................... 120

XXI. JOHN MEINE, JUNR., STUDENT OF DIVINITY .......... 126

XXII. ALEXANDER BRODIE OF BRODIE ......................... 131

XXIII. JOHN FLEMING, BAILIE OF LEITH ....................... 139

XXIV. THE PARISHIONERS OF KILMACOLM ....................146

# SAMUEL RUTHERFORD

BY

Alexander Whyte

# I. JOSHUA REDIVIVUS

'He sent me as a spy to see the land and to try the ford.'
*Rutherford*.

Samuel Rutherford, the author of the seraphic *Letters*, was born in the south of Scotland in the year of our Lord 1600. Thomas Goodwin was born in England in the same year, Robert Leighton in 1611, Richard Baxter in 1615, John Owen in 1616, John Bunyan in 1628, and John Howe in 1630. A little vellum-covered volume now lies open before me, the title-page of which runs thus:--'Joshua Redivivus, or Mr. Rutherford's Letters, now published for the use of the people of God: but more particularly for those who now are, or may afterwards be, put to suffering for Christ and His cause. By a well-wisher to the work and to the people of God. Printed in the year 1664.' That is all. It would not have been safe in 1664 to say more. There is no editor's name on the title-page, no publisher's name, and no place of printing or of publication. Only two texts of forewarning and reassuring Scripture, and then the year of grace 1664.

Joshua Redivivus: That is to say, Moses' spy and pioneer, Moses' successor and the captain of the Lord's covenanted host come back again. A second Joshua sent to Scotland to go before God's people in that land and in that day; a spy who would both by his experience and by his testimony cheer and encourage the suffering people of God. For all this Samuel Rutherford truly was. As he said of himself in one of his letters to Hugh Mackail, he was indeed a spy sent out to make experiment upon the life of silence and separation, banishment and martyrdom, and to bring back a report of that life for the vindication of Christ and for the support and encouragement of His people. It was a happy thought of Rutherford's first editor, Robert M'Ward, his old Westminster Assembly secretary, to put at the top of his title-page, Joshua risen again from the dead, or, Mr. Rutherford's Letters written from his place of banishment in Aberdeen.

In selecting his twelve spies, Moses went on the principle of choosing the best and the ablest men he could lay hold of in all Israel. And in selecting Samuel Rutherford to be the first sufferer for His covenanted people in Scotland, our Lord took a man who was already famous for his character and his services. For no man of his age in broad Scotland stood higher as a scholar, a theologian, a controversialist, a preacher and a very saint than Samuel Rutherford. He had been settled at Anwoth on the Solway in 1627, and for the next nine years he had lived such a noble life among his people as to make Anwoth famous as long as Jesus Christ has a Church in Scotland. As we say Bunyan and Bedford, Baxter and Kidderminster, Newton and Olney, Edwards and Northampton, Boston and Ettrick, M'Cheyne and St. Peter's, so we say Rutherford and Anwoth.

His talents, his industry, his scholarship, his preaching power, his pastoral solicitude and his saintly character all combined to make Rutherford a marked man both to the friends and to the enemies of the truth. His talents and his industry while he was yet a student in Edinburgh had carried him to the top of his classes, and all his days he could write in Latin better than either in Scotch or English. His habits of work at Anwoth soon became a very proverb. His people boasted that their minister was always at his books, always among his parishioners, always at their sick-beds and their death-beds, always catechising their children and always alone with his God. And then the matchless preaching of the parish church of Anwoth. We can gather what made the Sabbaths of Anwoth so memorable both to Rutherford and to his people from the books we still have from those great Sabbaths: *The Trial and the Triumph of Faith*; *Christ Dying and Drawing Sinners to Himself*; and such like. Rutherford was the 'most moving and the most affectionate of preachers,' a preacher determined to know nothing but Jesus Christ and Him crucified, but not so much crucified, as crucified and risen again--crucified indeed, but now glorified. Rutherford's life for his people at Anwoth has something altogether superhuman and unearthly about it. His correspondents in his own day and his critics in our day stumble at his too intense devotion to his charge; he lived for his congregation, they tell us, almost to the neglect of his wife and children. But by the time of his banishment his home was desolate, his wife and children were in the grave. And all the time and thought and love they had got from him while they were alive had, now that they were dead, returned with new and intensified devotion to his people and his parish.

> Fair Anwoth by the Solway,
>   To me thou still art dear,
> E'en from the verge of heaven
>   I drop for thee a tear.
>
> Oh! if one soul from Anwoth
>   Meet me at God's right hand,
> My heaven will be two heavens
>   In Immanuel's Land.

This then was the spy chosen by Jesus Christ to go out first of all the ministers of Scotland into the life of banishment in that day, so as to try its fords and taste its vineyards, and to report to God's straitened and persecuted people at home.

To begin with, it must always be remembered that Rutherford was not laid in irons in Aberdeen, or cast into a dungeon. He was simply deprived of his pulpit and of his liberty to preach, and was sentenced to live in silence in the town of Aberdeen. Like Dante, another great spy of God's providence and grace, Rutherford was less a prisoner than an exile. But if any man thinks that simply to be an exile is a small punishment, or a light cross, let him read the psalms and prophecies of Babylon, the *Divine Comedy*, and Rutherford's *Letters*. Yes, banishment was banishment; exile was exile; silent Sabbaths were silent Sabbaths; and a borrowed fireside with all its willing heat was still a borrowed fireside; and, spite of all that the best people of Aberdeen could do for Samuel Rutherford, he felt the friendliest stairs of that city to be very steep to his feet, and its best bread to be very salt in his mouth.

But, with all that, Samuel Rutherford would have been but a blind and unprofitable spy for the best people of God in Scotland, for Marion M'Naught, and Lady Kenmure, and Lady Culross, for the Cardonesses, father, and mother, and son, and for Hugh Mackail, and such like, if he had tasted nothing more bitter than borrowed bread in Aberdeen, and climbed nothing steeper than a granite stair. 'Paul had need,' Rutherford writes to Lady Kenmure, 'of the devil's service to buffet him, and far more, you and me.' I am downright afraid to go on to tell you how Satan was sent to buffet Samuel Rutherford in his banishment, and how he was sifted as wheat is sifted in his exile. I would not expose such a saint of God to every eye, but I look for fellow-worshippers here on these Rutherford Sabbath evenings, who know something of the plague of their own hearts, and who are comforted in their banishment and battle by nothing more than when they are assured that they are not alone in the deep darkness. 'When Christian had travelled in this disconsolate condition for some time he thought he heard the voice of a man as going before him and saying, " *Though I walk through the Valley of the Shadow of Death I will fear no ill, for Thou art with me*." Then he was glad, and that for these reasons:--Firstly, because he gathered from thence that some one who feared God was in this valley as well as himself. Secondly, for that he perceived that God was with them though in that dark and dismal state; and why not, thought he, with me? Thirdly, for that he hoped, could he overtake them, to have company by and by.' And, in like manner, I am certain that it will encourage and save from despair some who now hear me if I just report to them some of the discoveries and experiences of himself that Samuel Rutherford made among the siftings and buffetings of his Aberdeen exile. Writing to Lady Culross, he says:--'O my guiltiness, the follies of my youth and the neglects of my calling, they all do stare me in the face here; . . . the world hath sadly mistaken me: no man knoweth what guiltiness is in me.' And to Lady Boyd, speaking of some great lessons he had learnt in the school of adversity, he says, 'In the third place, I have seen here my abominable vileness, and it is such that if I were well known no one in all the kingdom would ask me how I do. . . . I am a deeper hypocrite and a shallower professor than any one could believe. Madam, pity me, the chief of sinners.' And, again, to the Laird of Carlton: 'Woe, woe is me, that men should think there is anything in me. The house-devils that keep me company and this sink of corruption make me to carry low sails. . . . But, howbeit I am a wretched captive of sin, yet my Lord can hew heaven out of worse timber than I am, if worse there be.' And to Lady Kenmure: 'I am somebody in the books of my friends, . . . but there are armies of thoughts within me, saying the contrary, and laughing at the mistakes of my many friends. Oh! if my inner side were only seen!' Ah no, my brethren, no land is so fearful to them that are sent to search it out as their own heart. 'The land,' said the ten spies, 'is a land that eateth up the inhabitants thereof; the cities are walled up to heaven, and very great, and the children of Anak dwell in them. We were in their sight as grasshoppers, and so we were in our own sight.' Ah, no! no stair is so steep as the stair of sanctification, no bread is so salt as that which is baked for a man of God out of the wild oats of his past sin and his present sinfulness. Even Joshua and Caleb, who brought back a good report of the land, did not deny that the children of Anak were there, or that their walls went up to heaven, or that they, the spies, were as grasshoppers before their foes: Caleb and Joshua only said that, in spite of all that, if the Lord delighted in His people, He both could and would give them a land flowing with milk and honey. And be it recorded and remembered to his credit and his praise that, with all his self-discoveries and self- accusings, Rutherford did not utter one single word of doubt or despair; so far from that was he, that in one of his letters to Hugh M'Kail he tells us that some of his correspondents have written to him that he is possibly too joyful under the cross. Blunt old Knockbrex, for one, wrote to his old minister to restrain somewhat his ecstasy. So true was it, what Rutherford said of himself to David Dickson, that he was 'made up of extremes.' So he was, for I know no man among all my masters in personal religion who unites greater extremes in himself than Samuel Rutherford. Who weeps like Rutherford over his banishment from Anwoth, while all the time who is so feasted in Christ's palace in Aberdeen? Who loathes himself like Rutherford? Not Bunyan, not Brea, not Boston; and, at the same time, who is so transported and lost to himself in the beauty and sweetness of Christ? As we read his raptures we almost say with cautious old Knockbrex, that possibly Rutherford is somewhat too full of ecstasy for this fallen, still unsanctified, and still so slippery world.

It took two men to carry back the cluster of grapes the spies cut down at Esh-col, and there is sweetness and strength and ecstasy enough for ten men in any one of Rutherford's inebriated Letters. 'See what the land is, and whether it be fat or lean, and bring back of the fruits of the land.' This was the order given by Moses to the twelve spies. And, whether the land was fat or lean, Moses and all Israel could judge for themselves when the spies laid down their load of grapes at Moses' feet. 'I can report nothing but good of the land,' said Joshua Redivivus, as he sent back such clusters of its vineyards and such pots of its honey to Hugh Mackail, to Marion M'Naught, and to Lady Kenmure.  And then, when all his letters were collected and published, never surely, since the Epistles of Paul and the Gospel of John, had such clusters of encouragement and such intoxicating cordials been laid to the lips of the Church of Christ.

Our old authors tell us that after the northern tribes had tasted the warmth and the sweetness of the wines of Italy they could take no rest till they had conquered and taken possession of that land of sunshine where such grapes so plentifully grew. And how many hearts have been carried captive with the beauty and the grace of Christ, and with the land of Immanuel, where He drinks wine with the saints in His Father's house, by the reading of Samuel Rutherford's Letters, the day of the Lord will alone declare.

> Oh! Christ He is the Fountain,
>    The deep sweet Well of love!
> The streams on earth I've tasted,
>    More deep I'll drink above.
> There to an ocean fulness
>    His mercy doth expand,
> And glory, glory dwelleth
>    In Immanuel's Land.

## II. SAMUEL RUTHERFORD AND SOME
## OF HIS EXTREMES

'I am made of extremes.'-- *Rutherford*.

A story is told in Wodrow of an English merchant who had occasion to visit Scotland on business about the year 1650. On his return home his friends asked him what news he had brought with him from the north. 'Good news,' he said; 'for when I went to St. Andrews I heard a sweet, majestic- looking man, and he showed me the majesty of God. After him I heard a little fair man, and he showed me the loveliness of Christ. I then went to Irvine, where I heard a well-favoured, proper old man with a long beard, and that man showed me all my own heart.' The little fair man who showed this English merchant the loveliness of Christ was Samuel Rutherford, and the proper old man who showed him all his own heart was David Dickson. Dr. M'Crie says of David Dickson that he was singularly successful in dissecting the human heart and in winning souls to the Redeemer, and all that we know of Dickson bears out that high estimate. When he was presiding on one occasion at the ordination of a young minister, whom he had had some hand in bringing up, among the advices the old minister gave the new beginner were these:--That he should remain unmarried for four years, in order to give himself up wholly to his great work; and that both in preaching and in prayer he should be as succinct as possible so as not to weary his hearers; and, lastly, 'Oh, study God well and your own heart.' We have five letters of Rutherford's to this master of the human heart, and it is in the third of these that Rutherford opens his heart to his father in the Gospel, and tells him that he is made up of extremes.

In every way that was so. It is a common remark with all Rutherford's biographers and editors and commentators what extremes met in that little fair man. The finest thing that has ever been written on Rutherford is Mr. Taylor Innes's lecture in the Evangelical Succession series. And the intellectual extremes that met in Rutherford are there set forth by Rutherford's acute and sympathetic critic at some length. For one thing, the greatest speculative freedom and theological breadth met in Rutherford with the greatest ecclesiastical hardness and narrowness. I do not know any author of that day, either in England or in Scotland, either Prelatist or Puritan, who shows more imaginative freedom and speculative power than Ruther-ford does in his **Christ Dying**, unless it is his still greater contemporary, Thomas Goodwin. And it is with corresponding distress that we read some of Rutherford's polemical works, and even the polemical parts of his heavenly Letters. There is a remarkable passage in one of his controversial books that reminds us of some of Shakespeare's own tributes to England: 'I judge that in England the Lord hath many names and a fair company that shall stand at the side of Christ when He shall render up the kingdom to the Father; and that in that renowned land there be men of all ranks, wise, valorous, generous, noble, heroic, faithful, religious, gracious, learned.' Rutherford's whole passage is worthy to stand beside Shakespeare's great passage on 'this blessed plot, this earth, this realm, this England.' But persecution from England and controversy at home so embittered Rutherford's sweet and gra-cious spirit that passages like that are but few and far between. But let him away out into pure theology, and, especially, let him get his wings on the person, and the work, and the glory of Christ, and few theologians of any age or any school rise to a larger air, or command a wider scope, or discover a clearer eye of speculation than Rutherford, till we feel exactly like the laird of Glanderston, who, when Rutherford left a controversial passage in a sermon and went on to speak of Christ, cried out in the church--'Ay, hold you there, minister; you are all right there!' A domestic controversy that arose in the Church of Scotland towards the end of Rutherford's life so separated Rutherford from Dickson and Blair that Rutherford would not take part with Blair, the 'sweet, majestic-looking man,' in the Lord's Supper. 'Oh, to be above,' Blair exclaimed, 'where there are no misunderstandings!' It was this same controversy that made John Livingstone say in a letter to Blair that his wife and he had had more bitterness over that dispute than ever they had tasted since they knew what bitterness meant. Well might Rutherford say, on another such occasion, 'It is hard when saints rejoice in the sufferings of saints, and when the redeemed hurt, and go nigh to hate the redeemed.' Watch and pray, my brethren, lest in controversy--ephemeral and immaterial controversy--you also go near to hate and hurt one another, as Rutherford did.

And then, what strength, combined with what tenderness, there is in Rutherford! In all my acquaintance with literature I do not know any author who has two books under his name so unlike one another, two books that are such a contrast to one another, as *Lex Rex* and the *Letters*. A more firmly built argument than *Lex Rex*, an argument so clamped together with the iron bands of scholastic and legal lore, is not to be met with in any English book; a more lawyer-looking production is not in all the Advocates' Library than just *Lex Rex*. There is as much emotion in the multiplication table as there is in *Lex Rex*; and then, on the other hand, the *Letters* have no other fault but this, that they are overcharged with emotion. The *Letters* would be absolutely perfect if they were only a little more restrained and chastened in this one respect. The pundit and the poet are the opposites and the extremes of one another; and the pundit and the poet meet, as nowhere else that I know of, in the author of *Lex Rex* and the *Letters*.

Then, again, what extremes of beauty and sweetness there are in Rutherford's style, too often intermingled with what carelessness and disorder. What flashes of noblest thought, clothed in the most apt and well-fitting words, on the same page with the most slatternly and down-at- the-heel English. Both Dr. Andrew Bonar and Dr. Andrew Thomson have given us selections from Rutherford's *Letters* that would quite justify us in claiming Rutherford as one of the best writers of English in his day; but then we know out of what thickets of careless composition these flowers have been collected. Both Gillespie and Rutherford ran a tilt at Hooker; but alas for the equipment and the manners of our champions when compared with the shining panoply and the knightly grace of the author of the incomparable *Polity*.

And then, morally, as great extremes met in Rutherford as intellectually. Newman has a fine sermon under a fine title, 'Saintliness not forfeited by the Penitent.' 'No degree of sin,' he says, 'precludes the acquisition of any degree of holiness, however high. No sinner so great, but he may, through God's grace, become a saint ever so great.' And then he goes on to illustrate that, and balance that, and almost to retract and deny all that, in a way that all his admirers only too well know. But still it stands true. A friend of mine once told me that it was to him often the most delightful and profitable of Sabbath evening exercises just to take down Newman's sermons and read their titles over again. And this mere title, I feel sure, has encouraged and comforted many: 'Saintliness not forfeited by the Penitent.' And Samuel Rutherford's is just another great name to be added to the noble roll of saintly penitents we all have in our minds taken out of Scripture and Church History. Neither great Saintliness nor great service was forfeited by this penitent; and he is constantly telling us how the extreme of demerit and the extreme of gracious treatment met in him; how he had at one time destroyed himself, and how God had helped him; how, where sin had abounded, grace had abounded much more. In one of the very last letters he ever wrote--his letter to James Guthrie in 1661--he is still amazed that God has not brought his sin to the Market Cross, to use his own word. But all through his letters this same note of admiration and wonder runs--that he has been taken from among the pots and his wings covered with silver and gold. Truly, in his case the most seraphic Saintliness was not forfeited, and we who read his books may well bless God it was so.

And then, experimentally also, what extremes met in our author! Pascal in Paris and Rutherford in Anwoth and St. Andrews were at the very opposite poles ecclesiastically from one another. I do not like to think what Rutherford would have said of Pascal, but I cannot embody what I have to say of Rutherford's experimental extremes better than just by this passage taken from the *Thoughts*: 'The Christian religion teaches the righteous man that it lifts him even to a participation in the divine nature; but that, in this exalted state, he still bears within him the fountain of all corruption, which renders him during his whole life subject to error and misery, to sin and death, while at the same time it proclaims to the most wicked that they can still receive the grace of their Redeemer.' And again, 'Did we not know ourselves full of pride, ambition, lust, weakness, misery and injustice, we were indeed blind. . . . What then can we feel but a great esteem for a religion that is so well acquainted with the defects of man, and a great desire for the truth of a religion that promises remedies so precious.' And yet again, what others thought of him, and how they treated him, compared with what he knew himself to be, caused Rutherford many a bitter reflection. Every letter he got consulting him and appealing to him as if he had been God's living oracle made him lie down in the very dust with shame and self-abhorrence. Writing on one occasion to Robert Blair he told him that his letter consulting him about some matter of Christian experience had been like a blow in the face to him; it affects me much, said Rutherford, that a man like you should have any such opinion of me. And, apologising for his delay in replying to a letter of Lady Boyd's, he says that he is put out of all love of writing letters because his correspondents think things about him that he himself knows are not true. 'My white side comes out on paper--but at home there is much black work. All the challenges that come to me are true.' There was no man then alive on the earth so much looked up to and consulted in the deepest matters of the soul, in the secrets of the Lord with the soul, as Rutherford was, and his letters bear evidence on every page that there was no man who had a more loathsome and a more hateful experience of his own heart, not even Taylor, not even Owen, not even Bunyan, not even Baxter. What a day of extremest men that was, and what an inheritance we extreme men have had left us, in their inward, extreme, and heavenly books!

Once more, hear him on the tides of feeling that continually rose and fell within his heart. Writing from Aberdeen to Lady Boyd, he says: 'I have not now, of a long time, found such high springtides as formerly. The sea is out, and I cannot buy a wind and cause it to flow again; only I wait on the shore till the Lord sends a full sea. . . . But even to dream of Him is sweet.' And then, just over the leaf, to Marion M'Naught: 'I am well: honour to God. . . . He hath broken in upon a poor prisoner's soul like the swelling of Jordan. I am bank and brim full: a great high springtide of the consolations of Christ hath overwhelmed me.' . . . But sweet as it is to read his rapturous expressions when the tide is full, I feel it far more helpful to hear how he still looks and waits for the return of the tide when the tide is low, and when the shore is full, as all left shores are apt to be, of weeds and mire, and all corrupt and unclean things. Rutherford is never more helpful to his correspondents than when they consult him about their ebb tides, and find that he himself either has been, or still is, in the same experience.

But why do we disinter such texts as this out of such an author as Samuel Rutherford? Why do we tell to all the world that such an eminent saint was full of such sad extremes? Well, we surely do so out of obedience to the divine command to comfort God's people; for, next to their having no such extremes in themselves, their next best comfort is to be told that great and eminent saints of God have had the very same besetting sins and staggering extremes as they still have. If the like of Samuel Rutherford was vexed and weakened with such intellectual contradictions and spiritual extremes in his mind, in his heart and in his history, then may we not hope that some such saintliness, if not some such service as his, may be permitted to us also?

---

## III.  MARION M'NAUGHT

'O woman beloved of God.'-- *Rutherford*.

The world knows nothing of its greatest men,' says Sir Henry Taylor in his ***Philip Van Artevelde***; and it knows much less of its greatest women. I have not found Marion M'Naught's name once mentioned outside of Samuel Rutherford's Letters. But she holds a great place--indeed, the foremost place--in that noble book, to be written in which is almost as good as to be written in heaven.

Rutherford's first letter to Marion M'Naught was written from the manse of Anwoth on the 6th of June 1627, and out of a close and lifelong correspondence we are happy in having had preserved to us some forty-five of Rutherford's letters to his first correspondent. But, most unfortunately, we have none of her letters back again to Anwoth or Aberdeen or London or St. Andrews. It is much to be wished we had, for Marion M'Naught was a woman greatly gifted in mind, as well as of quite exceptional experience even for that day of exceptional experiences in the divine life. But we can almost construct her letters to Rutherford for ourselves, so pointedly and so elaborately and so affectionately does Rutherford reply to them.

Marion M'Naught is already a married woman, and the mother of three well-grown children, when we make her acquaintance in Rutherford's Letters. She had sprung of an ancient and honourable house in the south of Scotland, and she was now the wife of a well-known man in that day, William Fullarton, the Provost of Kirkcudbright. It is interesting to know that Marion M'Naught was closely connected with Lady Kenmure, another of Rutherford's chief correspondents. Lord Kenmure was her mother's brother. Kenmure had lived a profligate and popularity-hunting life till he was laid down on his death-bed, when he underwent one of the most remarkable conversions anywhere to be read of--a conversion that, as it would appear, his niece Marion M'Naught had no little to do with. As long as Kenmure was young and well, as long as he was haunting the purlieus of the Court, and selling his church and his soul for a smile from the King, the Provost of Kirkcudbright and his saintly wife were despised and forgotten; but when he was suddenly brought face to face with death and judgment, when his ribbons and his titles were now like the coals of hell in his conscience, nothing would satisfy him but that his niece must leave her husband and her children and take up her abode in Kenmure Castle. *The Last and Heavenly Speeches of Lord Kenmure* was a classic memoir of those days, and in that little book we read of his niece's constant attendance at his bedside, as good a nurse for his soul as she was for his body.

Samuel Rutherford's favourite correspondent was, to begin with, a woman of quite remarkable powers of mind. We gather that impression powerfully as we read deeper and deeper into the remarkable series of letters that Rutherford addressed to her. To no one does he go into deeper matters both of Church and State, both of doctrinal and personal religion than to her, and the impression of mental power as well as of personal worth she made on Rutherford, she must have made on many of the ablest and best men of that day. Robert Blair, for instance, tells us that when he was on his way home from London to Ireland he visited Scotland chiefly that he might see Rutherford at Anwoth and Marion M'Naught at Kirkcudbright, and when he came to Kirkcudbright he found Rutherford also there. And when Rutherford was in exile in Aberdeen, and in deep anxiety about his people at Anwoth, he wrote beseeching Marion M'Naught to go to Anwoth and give his people her counsel about their congregational and personal affairs. But, above all, it is from the depth and the power of Rutherford's letters to herself on the inward life that we best gather the depth and the power of this remarkable woman's mind.

There is no other subject of thought that gives such scope for the greatest gifts of the human mind as does the life of God in the soul. There is no book in all the world that demands such a combination of mental gifts and spiritual graces to understand it aright as the Bible. The history and the biography of the Bible, the experimental parts of the Bible, the doctrines of grace deduced by the apostles out of the history and the experience recorded in the Bible, and then the personal, the most inward and most spiritual bearing of all that,--what occupation can be presented to the mind of man or woman to compare with that? True religion, really true religion, gives unequalled and ever-increasing scope for the best gifts of mind and for the best graces of heart and character. 'In truth, religious obedience is a very intricate problem, and the more so the farther we proceed in it.' And he has poor eyes and a poor heart for true religion, and for its best fruits both in the mind and the heart and the character, who does not see those fruits increasing letter by letter as Rutherford writes to Marion M'Naught.

Her public spirit also made Marion M'Naught to be held in high honour. Her husband was a public man, and his intelligent fidelity to truth and justice in that day made his name far more public than ever he wished it to be. And in all his services and sufferings for the truth he had a splendid wife in Marion M'Naught. 'Remember me to your husband,' Rutherford writes; 'tell him that Christ is worthy to be suffered for not only to blows but to blood. He will find that innocence and uprightness will hold his feet firm and make him happy when jouking will not do it.' And again, 'Encourage your husband and tell him that truth will yet keep the crown of the causey in Scotland.' And when the petition is being got up for his being permitted to return to Anwoth, Rutherford asks his correspondent to procure that three or four hundred noblemen, gentlemen, countrymen and citizens shall be got to subscribe it--a telling tribute, surely, to her public spirit and her great influence.

But an independent mind and a public spirit like hers could not exist in those days, or in any day this world has yet seen, without raising up many and bitter enemies. And both she and her husband suffered heavily, both in name and in estate, from the malice and the hatred that their fearless devotion to truth and justice stirred up. So much so, that some of the finest passages in Rutherford's early letters to her are those in which he counsels her and her husband to patience, and meekness, and forgiveness of injuries. 'Keep God's covenant in all your trials. Hold you by His blessed word, and sin not; flee anger, wrath, grudging, envying, fretting. Forgive an hundred pence to your fellow-servant, for your Lord has forgiven you ten thousand talents.' And again: 'Be patient; Christ went to heaven with many a wrong. His visage was more marred than that of any of the sons of men. He was wronged and received no reparation, but referred all to that day when all wrongs shall be righted.' And again: 'You live not upon men's opinion. Happy are you if, when the world trampleth upon you in your credit and good name, you are yet the King's gold and stamped with His image. Pray for the spirit of love, for love beareth all things, believeth all things, hopeth all things, endureth all things. Forgive, therefore, your fellow-servant his one talent. Always remember what has been forgiven you.' And on every page of the Kirkcudbright correspondence we see that, amid all these temptations and trials, no man had a better wife than the provost, and no children a better mother than Grizel and her two brothers. Her talents sought no nobler sphere for their exercise and increase than her own fireside; and her public spirit was better seen in her life at home than anywhere out of doors. Hers was truly a public spirit, and like a spirit it inspired and animated both her own and her husband's life with interest in and with care for the best good, both of the Church and the State. Her public spirit was not incompatible with great personal modesty and humility, and great attention to her domestic duties, all rooted in a life hid with Christ in God.

And then, all this--her birth, her station, her talents, and her public spirit-- could not fail to give her a great influence for good. In a single line of Rutherford's on this subject, we see her whole lifetime: 'You are engaged so in God's work in Kirkcudbright that if you remove out of that town all will be undone.' What a tribute is that to the provost's wife! And again, far on in the Letters he writes to Grizel Fullarton: 'Your dear mother, now blessed and perfected with glory, kept life in that place, and my desire is that you succeed her in that way.' What a pride to have such a mother; and what a tradition for a daughter to take up! So have we all known in country towns and villages one man or one woman who kept life in the place. Out of the memories of my own boyhood there rises up, here a minister and there a farmer, here a cloth- merchant and there a handloom weaver, here a blacksmith's wife and there a working housekeeper, who kept life in the whole place. It is not station that does it, nor talent, though both station and talent greatly help; it is character, it is true and genuine godliness. True and genuine godliness-- especially when it is purged of pride, and harsh judgment, and too much talk, and is adorned with humility and meekness, and all the other fruits of holy love--true and pure godliness in a most obscure man or woman will find its way to a thousand consciences, and will impress and overawe a whole town, as Marion M'Naught's rare godliness impressed and overawed all Kirkcudbright. Just as, on the other hand, the ignorance, the censoriousness, the bitterness, the intolerance, that too often accompany what would otherwise be true godliness, work as widespread mischief as true godliness works good. 'One little deed done for God's sake, and against our natural inclination, though in itself only of a conceding or passive character, to brook an insult, to face a danger, or to resign an advantage, has in it a power outbalancing all the dust and chaff of mere profession--the profession whether of enlightened benevolence or candour, or, on the other hand, of high religious faith and fervent zeal;' or, as Rutherford could write to Marion M'Naught's daughter: 'There is a wide and deep difference between a name of godliness and the power of godliness.' Even the schoolboys of Kirkcudbright could quite well distinguish the name from the reality; and long after they were Christian men they would tell with reverence and with love when, and from whom, they took their first and never-to-be-forgotten impressions. It was, they would say to their children, from that woman of such rare godliness as well as public spirit, Marion M'Naught.

It was all this, and nothing other and nothing less than all this, that made Marion M'Naught Rutherford's favourite correspondent. Her mind and her heart together early and often drew her across the country to Rutherford's preaching. Marion M'Naught had a good minister of her own at home; but Rutherford was Rutherford, and he made Anwoth Anwoth. I think I can understand something of her delight on Communion forenoons, when his text was Christ Dying, in John xii. 32, or the Syro-Phoenician woman, in Matt. xv. 28. And then the feasts on the fast-days at Kirkcudbright, over the cloud of witnesses, in Heb. xii. 1, and all tears wiped away, in Rev. xxi. 4, and the marriage of the Lamb, in xix. 7. And then, on the other hand, Rutherford is not surely to be blamed for loving such a hearer. His Master loved a Mary also of His day, for that also among other good reasons. If a good hearer likes a good preacher, why should a good preacher not like a good hearer? Take a holiday, and give us another day soon of such and such a preacher, our people sometimes say to us. And why should that preacher not also say to us, Give me a day soon again of your good hearers? As a matter of fact, our good preaching friends do say that to us. And why not? Fine hearers, deep hearers, thoroughly well-prepared hearers, hearers of genius are almost as scarce as fine, deep, thoroughly well-prepared preachers and preachers of genius. And who shall blame Rutherford for liking to see Marion M'Naught coming into the church on a Sabbath morning as well as she liked to see him coming into the pulpit? 'I go to Anwoth so often,' she said, 'because, though other ministers show me the majesty of God and the plague of my own heart, Mr. Samuel does both these things, but he also shows me, as no other minister ever does, the loveliness of Christ.' It is as great a mistake to think that all our Christian people are able to take in a sermon on the loveliness of Christ as it is that all ordained men can preach such a sermon. There are diversities of gifts among hearers as well as among preachers; and when the gifts of the pulpit meet the corresponding graces in the pew, you need not wonder that they recognise and delight in one another. Jesus Christ was Rutherford's favourite subject in the pulpit, and thus it was that he was Marion M'Naught's favourite preacher, as she, again, was his favourite hearer in the church and his favourite correspondent in the Letters. To how many in this house to-night could a preacher say that he wished them all to be 'over head and ears in love to Christ'? What preacher could say a thing like that in truth and soberness? And how many could hear it? Only a preacher of the holy passion of Rutherford, and only a hearer of the intellect and heart and rare experience of Marion M'Naught. 'O the fair face of the man Jesus Christ!' he cries out. And again: 'O time, time, why dost thou move so slowly! Come hither, O love of Christ! What astonishment will be mine when I first see that fairest and most lovely face! It would be heaven to me just to look through a hole of heaven's door to see Christ's countenance!' No wonder that the congregations were few, and the correspondents who could make anything of a man of such a 'fanatic humour' as that! But, then, no wonder, on the other hand, that, when two fanatics so full of that humour as Samuel Rutherford and Marion M'Naught met, they corresponded ever after with one another in their own enraptured language night and day.

# IV. LADY KENMURE

'Build your nest, Madam, upon no tree here, for God hath sold this
whole forest to death.'-- **Rutherford**.

Lady Kenmure was one of the Campbells of Argyll, a family distinguished
for the depth of their piety, their public spirit, and their love for the Presbyterian polity; and Lady Jane was one of the most richly-gifted members
of that richly-gifted house. But, with all that, Lady Jane Campbell had her
own crosses to carry. She had the sore cross of bad health to carry all her days.
Then she had the sad misfortune to make a very bad marriage in the morning of her
days; and, partly as the result of all that, and partly because of her peculiar mental
constitution, her whole life was drenched with a deep melancholy. But, as we are
told in John Howie and elsewhere, all these evils and misfortunes were made to
work together for good to her through the special grace of God, and through the
wise and wistful care of her lifelong friend and minister and correspondent, Samuel
Rutherford. Lady Jane Campbell had very remarkable gifts of mind. We would
have expected that from her distinguished pedigree; and we have abundant proof
of that in Rutherford's sheaf of letters to her. His dedication of that most remarkable piece, *The Trial and Triumph of Faith*, is sufficient of itself to show how
highly Rutherford esteemed Lady Kenmure, both as to her head and her heart. Till
our theological students have been led to study *The Trial and Triumph of Faith:*
*Christ Dying and Drawing Sinners to Himself*--which, to my mind, is by far the
best of Rutherford's works-- *The Covenant of Grace* and *The Influences of Grace*,
they will have no conception of the intellectual rank of Samuel Rutherford himself,
or of the intelligence and the attainments of his hearers and readers and correspondents. Thomas Goodwin was always telling the theological students of Oxford in

those days to thicken their too thin homilies with more doctrine: Rutherford's very thinnest books are almost too thick, both with theology and with thought.

How ever a woman like Jane Campbell came to marry a man like John Gordon will remain a mystery. It was not that he was a man of no mind; he was a man of no worth or interest of any kind. He was a rake and a lick-spittle, the very last man in Scotland for Jane Campbell to throw herself away upon. And she was too clever and too good a woman not to make a speedy and a heart-breaking discovery of the fatal mistake she had committed. Poor Jane Campbell soon wakened up to the discovery that she had exchanged the name and the family of a brave and noble house for the name and the house of a poltroon. No wonder that Rutherford's letters to her are so often headed: 'To Lady Kenmure, under illness and depression of mind.' Could you have kept quite well had you been a Campbell with John Gordon for a husband? Think of having to nurse your humbug of a husband through a shammed illness. Think of having to take a hand in sending in a sham doctor's certificate because your husband was too much of a time-server to go to Edinburgh to give his vote for a persecuted church. Think of having to wear the title and decoration your husband had purchased for you at the cost of his truth and honour and manhood. Lady Kenmure needed Samuel Rutherford's very best letters to help to keep her in bare life all the time the county dames were green with envy at the dear-bought honours. And Kenmure himself had to be brought to his death-bed before he became a husband worthy of his wife. We still read in his **Last Speeches** how God made Lord Gordon's sins to find him out, and with what firmness and with what tenderness Rutherford handled the soul of the dying man till all his cowardice, title-hunting, and truth- betraying life came back to his death-bed with a sharper sting in them than even his grossest sins. Whoredom and wine after all are but the lusts of a man, whereas time-serving and truth-selling are the lusts of a devil. 'Dig deeper,' said Rutherford to the dying courtier, and Kenmure did dig deeper, till he came down to the seals and the titles and the ribbons for which he had sold his soul. But he that confesses and forsakes his sins even at the eleventh hour shall always find mercy, and so it was with Lord Kenmure.

'Between the stirrup and the ground
Mercy I sought and mercy found.'

We do not grudge Viscount Kenmure all the grace he got from God; we shall need as much grace and more ourselves; but we do somewhat grudge such a man a place of honour among the Scots worthies. We are tempted to throw down the book and to demand what right John Gordon has to stand beside such men as Patrick Hamilton, and John Knox, and John Wishart, and Archibald Campbell, and Hugh M'Kail, and Richard Cameron, and Alexander Shields? But Lochgoin answers us that God sometimes accepts the late will for the whole timeous deed, and the bravery and loyalty of the wife for the meanness and poltroonery of the husband. 'Have you a present sense of God's love?' 'I have, I have,' said the dying Viscount. As Rutherford continued in prayer, Kenmure was observed to smile and look upwards. About sunset Lord Kenmure died, at the same instant that Rutherford said Amen to his prayer. *The Last and Heavenly Speeches* is a rare pamphlet that will well repay its price to him who will seek it out and read it.

This was the correspondent, then, to whom Samuel Rutherford wrote such counsels and encouragements as these: 'Therefore, madam, herein have comfort, that He who seeth perfectly through all your evils, and who knoweth the frame and constitution of your nature, and what is most healthful for your soul, holdeth every cup of affliction to your head with his own gracious hand. Never believe that your tender-hearted Saviour will mix your cup with one drachm-weight of poison. Drink, then, with the patience of the saints: wrestle, fight, go forward, watch, fear, believe, pray, and then you have all the infallible symptoms of one of the elect of Christ within you' (*Letter* III.). On the death of her infant daughter, Rutherford writes to the elect lady: 'She is only sent on before, like unto a star, which, going out of our sight, doth not die and vanish, but still shineth in another hemisphere. What she wanted of time she hath gotten of eternity, and you have now some plenishing up in heaven. Build your nest upon no tree here, for God hath sold the whole forest to death' (*Letter* IV.). 'Madam, when you are come to the other side of the water and have set down your foot on the shore of glorious eternity, and look back to the water and to your wearisome journey, and shall see in that clear glass of endless glory nearer to the bottom of God's wisdom, you shall then be forced to say, "If God had done otherwise with me than He hath done, I had never come to the enjoying of this crown of glory"' (*Letter* XL). 'Madam, tire not, weary not; for I dare find you the Son of God caution that when you are got up thither and have cast your eyes to view the golden city and the fair and never-withering Tree of Life that beareth twelve manner of fruits every month, you shall then say, "Four-and-twenty hours' abode in this place is worth threescore and ten years' sorrow upon earth"' (*Letter* XIX.). 'Your ladyship goeth on laughing and putting on a good countenance before the world, and yet you carry heaviness about with you. You do well, madam, not to make them witnesses of your grief who cannot be curers of it' (*Letter* XX.). 'Those who can take the crabbed tree of the cross handsomely upon their backs and fasten it on cannily shall find it such a burden as its wings are to a bird or its sails to a ship' (*Letter* LXIX.). 'I thought it had been an easy thing to be a Christian, and that to seek God had been at the next door; but, oh, the windings, the turnings, the ups and downs He hath led me through!' (*Letter* CIV.) 'I may be a book-man and yet be an idiot and a stark fool in Christ's way! The Bible beguiled the Pharisees, and so may I be misled' (*Letter* CVI.). 'I find you complaining of yourself, and it becometh a sinner so to do. I am not against you in that. The more sense the more life. The more sense of sin the less sin' (*Letter* CVI.). 'Seeing my sins and the sins of my youth deserved strokes, how am I obliged to my Lord who hath given me a waled and chosen cross! Since I must have chains, He would put golden chains on me, watered over with many consolations. Seeing I must have sorrow (for I have sinned, O Preserver of men!), He hath waled out for me joyful sorrow--honest, spiritual, glorious sorrow' (*Letter* CCVI.). There are hundreds of passages as good as these scattered up and down the forty-seven letters we have had preserved to us out of the large and intimate correspondence that passed between Samuel Rutherford and Lady Kenmure.

# V. LADY CARDONESS

'Think it not easy.'-- *Rutherford*.

What a lasting interest Samuel Rutherford's pastoral pen has given to the hoary old castle of Cardoness! Those nine so heart-winning letters that Rutherford wrote from Aberdeen to Cardoness Castle will still keep the memory of that old tower green long after its last stone has crumbled into dust. Readers of Rutherford's letters will long visit Cardoness Castle, and will musingly recall old John Gordon and Lady Cardoness, his wife, who both worked out each their own salvation in that old fortress, and found it a task far from easy. For nine faithful years Rutherford had been the anxious pastor of Cardoness Castle, and then, after he was banished from his pulpit and his parish, he only ministered to the Castle the more powerfully and prevailingly with his pen. After reading the Cardoness correspondence, we do not wonder to find the stout old chieftain heading the hard-fought battles which the people of Anwoth made both against Edinburgh and St. Andrews, when those cities and colleges attempted to take away their minister.

Rough old Cardoness had a warm place in his heart for Samuel Rutherford. The tough old pagan did not know how much he loved the little fair man with the high-set voice and the unearthly smile till he had lost him; and if force of arms could have kept Rutherford in Anwoth, Cardoness would soon have buckled on his sword. He was ashamed to be seen reading the letters that came to the Castle from Aberdeen; he denied having read them even after he had them all by heart. The wild old laird was nearer the Kingdom of Heaven than any one knew; even his Christian lady did not know all that Rutherford knew, and it was a frank sentence of Rutherford's in an Aberdeen letter that took lifelong hold of the old laird, and did more for his conversion and all that followed it than all Rutherford's sermons and all his other letters. 'I find true religion to be a hard task; I find heaven hard to be won,' wrote Rutherford to the old man; and that did more for his hard and late salvation than all the sermons he had ever heard. 'A hard task, a hard task!' the serving-men and the serving-women often overheard their old master muttering, as he alighted from the hunt and as he came home from his monthly visit to Edinburgh. 'A hard task!' he was often heard muttering, but no one to the day of his death ever knew all that his muttering meant.

'Read over your past life often,' Rutherford wrote to the old man. And Cardoness found that to be one of the hardest tasks he had ever tried. He had not forgotten his past life; there were things that came up out of his past continually that compelled him to remember it. But what Rutherford meant was that his old parishioner should willingly, deliberately and repeatedly open the stained and torn leaves of his past life and read it all over in the light of his old age, approaching death, and late-awakened conscience. Rutherford wished Cardoness to sit down as Matthew Henry says the captives sat down by the rivers of Babylon, and weep 'deliberate tears.' There were pages in his past life that it was the very pains of hell to old Cardoness to read; but he performed the hard task, and thus was brought much nearer salvation than even his old pastor knew. 'It will take a long lance to go to the bottom of your heart, my friend,' wrote Rutherford, faithfully, and, at the same time, most respectfully, to the old man. 'Human nature is lofty and head-strong in you, and it will cost you far more suffering to be mortified and sanctified than it costs the ordinary run of men.' And, instead of that plain speech offending or angering the old laird, it had the very opposite effect; it softened him, and humbled him, and encouraged him, and gave him new strength for the hard task on which he was day and night employed.

Cardoness was a small property, heavily bonded, and some of the leaves that were hardest to read in the diary of Gordon's early manhood told the bitter history of some added bonds. Sin would need to be sweet, for it is very dear. And then had come years of rack-renting of his tenants; the virtuous tenantry had to pay dearly for the vices of their lord. Rutherford had not been silent to old Cardoness about this matter in conversation, and he was not silent in his letters. 'You are now upon the very borders of the other life. I told you, when I was with you, the whole counsel of God in this matter, and I tell it you again. Awake to righteousness. Do not lay the burden of your house on other people; do not compel honest people to pay your old debts. Commit to memory 1 Sam. xii. 3, and ride out among your tenantry, my dear people, repeating, as you pass their stables and their cattle-stalls, "Behold, I am old and grey-headed; behold, here I am: whose ox have I taken? Whose ass have I taken? Whom have I defrauded? Whom have I oppressed?" I charge you to write to me here at once, and be plain with me, and tell me whether your salvation is sure. I hope for the best; but I know that your reckonings with the righteous Judge are both many and deep.' That was a hard task to set to a tyrannical old landlord who had been used to call no man master, or God either, to take such commands from a poor banished minister! But Cardoness did it. He mastered his rising pride and resentment and did it; and though he found it a hard task to go through with his reductions at next rent-day, yet he did it. Such boldness in the Day of Judgment will a good conscience give a man, as when old Cardoness actually stood up before the parishioners in the kirk of Anwoth and read to them, after the elders had conducted the exercises, a letter he had received last week from their silenced minister. It is one of Rutherford's longest and most passionate letters. Take a sentence or two out of it: 'My soul longeth exceedingly to hear whether there be any work of Christ in the parish that will bide the trial of fire and water. I think of my people in my sleep. You know how that, out of love to your souls, and out of the desire I had to make an honest account of you, I often testified my dislike of your ways, both in private and in public. Examine yourselves. I never knew so well what sin is as since I came to Aberdeen, though I was preaching about it every day to you. It would be life to me if you would read this letter to my people, and if they would profit by it. And now I write to thee, whoever thou art, O poor broken- hearted believer of the free salvation. Let Christ's atoning blood be on thy guilty soul. Christ has His heaven ready for thee, and He will make good His word before long. The blessing of a poor prisoner be upon you.'

Salvation was all this time proving itself to be a hard and ever harder task to John Gordon, with his proud neck, with his past life to read, with his debts and bonds and increasing expenditure, and with old age heavy upon him and death at his door. And Lady Cardoness was not finding her salvation to be easy either in all these untoward circumstances. 'Think it not easy,' wrote Rutherford to her. And to make her salvation sure, and to lead her to help her burdened husband with his hard task, Rutherford made bold to touch, though always tenderly and scripturally, upon the family cross. Their burdened and crowded estate lay between the whole Cardoness family and their salvation. Rutherford had seen that from the first day he arrived in Anwoth, and Cardoness and its difficulties lay heavy upon his heart in his prison in Aberdeen. And he could not write consolations and comforts and promises to Lady Cardoness till he had told her the truth again as he had told her husband. 'The kingdom of God and His righteousness is the one thing needful for you and for Cardoness and for your children,' wrote Rutherford. 'Houses, lands, credit, honour may all be lost if heaven is won. See that Cardoness and you buy the field where the pearl is. Sell all and buy that field. I beseech you to make conscience of your ways. Deal kindly with your tenants. I have written my mind at length to your husband, and my counsel to you is that, when his passion over-cometh him, a soft answer will turn away wrath. God casteth your husband often in my mind; I cannot forget him.'

What a power for good is in Samuel Rutherford's pen! At a few touches it carries us across Scotland to the mouth of the Fleet, and back two hundred and fifty years, and summons up Cardoness Castle, and peoples the hoary old keep again with John Gordon and his wife and children. We see the castle; we see the rack-rented farms lying around the rock on which the castle stands; we see Anwoth manse and pulpit empty and silenced; and then we see Rutherford dreaming about Cardoness as he sleeps in his far-off prison. The stout old laird rises before our eyes with more than his proper share of human nature--a mass of sinful manhood, strong in will, hot in temper, burdened with debt--debt in Edinburgh, and a deeper and darker debt elsewhere. The old lion lay, taken in a net of trouble, and the more he struggled the more entangled he became. And then her ladyship, a religious woman; yes, really a religious woman, only, like so many religious women, more religious than moral; more emotional than practically helpful in everyday life. All who have only heard of Samuel Rutherford and his letters will feel sure that he was just the effusive minister, and that his letters were just the soft stuff, to foster a piety that came out in feminine moods and emotions rather than in well-kept accounts and a well-managed kitchen and nursery. But we who have read Rutherford know better than that. Lady Cardoness is told, in kindest and sweetest but most unmistakable language, that she has to work out a not easy salvation in Cardoness Castle, and that, if her husband fails in his hard task, no small part of his blood will lie at her door.

But as we stand and look at Cardoness Castle, with its hard tasks for eternal life, a divine voice says to ourselves, Work out your own salvation with fear and trembling; and at that voice the old keep fades from our eyes, and our own house in modern Edinburgh rises up before us. Here, too, are old men with hard tasks between them and their salvation--a past life to read, to repent of, to redress, to reform, to weep deliberate and bitter tears over. There are debts and many other disorders that have to be put right; there are those under us--tenants and servants and poor relations--whose cases have to be dealt with considerately, justly, kindly, affectionately. There are things in those we love best--in a father, in a mother, in a husband, in a wife--that we have to be patient and forbearing with, and to command ourselves in the presence of Salvation was not easy in Cardoness Castle, with such a master, and such a mistress, and such children, and such tenants, and with such debts and straits of all kinds; and Cardoness Castle is repeated over and over again in hundreds of Edinburgh houses to-night.

---

# VI. LADY CULROSS

'Grace groweth best in winter.'-- **Rutherford**.

Elizabeth Melville was one of the ladies of the Covenant. It was a remarkable feature of a remarkable time in Scotland that so many ladies of birth,
intellect and influence were found on the side of the persecuted Covenanters. I do not remember any other period in the history of the Church of
Christ, since the day when the women of Galilee ministered of their substance
to our Lord Himself, in which noble women took such a noble part as did Lady
Culross, Lady Jane Campbell, the Duchess of Hamilton, the Duchess of Athol, and
other such ladies in that eventful time. We had something not unlike it again in the
ten years' conflict that culminated in the Disruption; and in the social and religious
movements of our own day, women of rank and talent are not found wanting. At
the same time, I do not know where to find such a cloud of witnesses for the faith
of Christ from among the eminent women of any one generation as Scotland can
show in her ladies of the Covenant.

Lady Culross's name will always be held in tender honour in the innermost
circles of our best Scottish Christians, for the hand she had in that wonderful outpouring of God's grace at the kirk of Shotts on that Thanksgiving Monday in 1636.
Under God, that Covenanters' Pentecost was more due to Lady Culross than to any
other human being. True, John Livingstone preached the Thanksgiving Sermon,
but it was through Lady Culross's influence that he was got to preach it; and he
preached it after a night of prayer spent by Lady Culross and her companions, such
that we read of next day's sermon and its success as a matter of course. I cannot ven-
ture to tell a heterogeneous audience the history of that night they spent at Shotts
with God. It is so unlike what we have ever seen or heard of. There may be one

or two of us here who have spent whole nights in prayer at some crisis in our life, going from one promise to another, when, in the Psalmist's words, the sorrows of death compassed us, and the pains of hell gat hold upon us. And we, one or two of us, may have had miracles from heaven forthwith performed upon us, fit to match in a private way with the hand of God on the kirk of Shotts. But even those of us who have such secrets between us and God, we, I fear, never spent a whole Communion night, never shutting our eyes but to pray for a baptism of spiritual blessing upon to-morrow's congregation. What a mother in Israel was Lady Culross, with five hundred children born of her travail in one day!

I have not found any of Lady Culross's letters to Samuel Rutherford, but John Livingstone's literary executors have published some eight letters she wrote to Livingstone, her close and lifelong friend. And Lady Culross's first letter to John Livingstone is in every point of view, a remarkable piece. It has a strength, an irony, and a tenderness in it that at once tell the reader that he is in the hands of a very remarkable writer. But it is not Lady Culross's literature that so much interests us and holds us, it is her religion; and it is its depth, its intensity, and the way it grows in winter. After a long and racy introduction, sometimes difficult to decipher, from its Fife idioms and obsolete spelling, she goes on thus: 'Did you get any heart to remember me and my bonds? As for me, I never found so great impediment within. Still, it is the Lord with whom we have to do, and He gives and takes, casts down and raises up, kills and makes alive as pleases His Majesty. . . . My task at home is augmented and tripled, and yet I fear worse. Sin in me and in mine is my greatest cross. I would, if it were the Lord's will, choose affliction rather than iniquity.-- Yours in C., E. MELVIL.'

It was now winter with John Livingstone. The persecution had overtaken him, and this is how her ladyship writes to him:--

'My very worthy and dear brother: Courage, dear brother: it is all in love, all works together for the best. You must be hewn and hammered and drest and prepared before you can be a *Leiving-ston* fit for His building. And if He is minded to make you meet to help others, you must look for another manner of strokes than you have yet felt, . . . but when you are laid low, and are vile in your own eyes, then He will raise you up and refresh you with some blinks of His favourable countenance, that you may be able to comfort others with those consolations wherewith you have been comforted of Him. . . . . Since God has put His work in your weak hands, look not for long ease here: you must feel the full weight of your calling: a weak man with a strong God. The pain is but a moment, the pleasure is everlasting, . . . cross upon cross: the end of one with me is but the beginning of another: but guiltiness in me and in mine is my greatest cross.' And after midnight one Sabbath she writes again to Livingstone: 'You cannot but say that the Lord was with you to-day; therefore, not only be content, but bless His name who put His word in your heart and in your mouth, and has overcome you with mercy when you deserved nothing but wrath, and has not only forgiven your many sins, but has saved you from breaking out, as it may be better men have done; but He has covered you and restrained you; has loved you freely and has made His saints to love you; who will guide you also with His counsel, and afterwards receive you to His glory.'

It was from his silent prison in Aberdeen that Samuel Rutherford wrote to Lady Culross the letter in which this sentence stands: 'I see that grace groweth best in winter.' Rutherford had had but a short and unsettled summer among the birds at Anwoth. His wife and his two children had been taken from him there, and now that which he loved more than wife or child had been taken from him too--his pulpit and pastoral work for Jesus Christ. He felt his banishment all the more keenly that he was the first of the evangelical ministers of Scotland to be so silenced. He will have plenty of companions in tribulation soon, if that will be any comfort to him; but, as it is, he confesses to Lady Culross that it was a peculiar pang to him to be 'the first in the kingdom put to utter silence.' The bitterness of banishment has been sung in immortal strains by Dante, whose grace under banishment also grew to a fruitfulness we still partake of to this day:--

> 'Thou shall leave each thing
> Beloved most dearly: this is the first shaft
> Shot from the bow of exile. Thou shall prove
> How salt the savour is of other's bread,
> How hard the passage to descend and climb
> By other's stairs. But that shall gall thee most
> Will be the worthless and vile company
> With whom thou must be thrown into these straits.'

But all this, to use a figure familiar among the Puritans of that day, only made Rutherford's true life return, like sap in winter, into its proper root, till we read in his later Aberdeen letters a rapture and a richness that his remain-at-home correspondents are fain to tone down.

Not only does true grace grow best in winter, but winter is the best season for planting grace. 'I was to be married, and she died,' was a young man's explanation to me the other day for proposing to sit down at the Lord's Table. The winter cold that carried off his future wife saw planted in his ploughed-up heart the seeds of divine grace; and, no doubt, all down the coming winters, with such short interludes of summers as may be before him in this cold climate, the grace that was planted in winter will grow. It is not a speculation, it is a personal experience that hundreds here can testify to, that the Bible, the Sabbath, the Supper, all became so many means of grace to them after some great affliction greatly sanctified. The death of a bride, the death of a wife, the death of a child; some blow from bride or wife or child worse than death; a lost hope quenched for ever--these, and things like these, are needful, as it would seem, to be suffered by most men before they will wholly open their hearts to the grace of God. 'Before I was afflicted I went astray: but now have I kept Thy word.'

At the same time, good and necessary as all such wintry experiences are, their good results on us do not last for ever. In too many cases they do not last long. It is rather a start in grace we take at such seasons than a steady and deep growth in it. The growth in grace that comes to us in connection with some sore affliction is apt to be violent and spasmodic; it comes and it goes with the affliction; it is not slow, constant, steady, sure, as all true and natural growth is. If one might say so, an unbroken winter in the soul, a continual inward winter, is needed to keep up a steady, deep and fruitful growth in grace. Now, is there anything in the spiritual husbandry of God that can be called such a winter of the soul? I think there is. The winter of our outward life--trials, crosses, sickness and death are all the wages of sin; and it is among these things that grace first strikes its roots. And what is the continual presence of sin in the soul but the true winter of the soul, amid which the grace that is planted in an outbreak of winter ever after strikes deeper root and grows? Once let a man be awakened of God to his own great sinfulness; and that not to its fruits in outward sorrow, but to its malignant roots that are twisted round and round and through and through his heart, and that man has thenceforth such a winter within him as shall secure to him a lifelong growth in the most inward grace. Once let a poor wretch awake to the unbroken winter of his own sinfulness, a sinfulness that is with him when he lies down and when he rises up, when he is abroad among men and when he is at home with himself alone: an incessant, increasing, agonising, overwhelming sense of sin,--and how that most miserable of men will grow in grace, and how he will drink in all the means of grace! How he will hear the word of grace preached, mixing it no longer with fault-finding, as he used to do, but with repentance and faith under any and every ministry. How he will examine himself every day; or, rather, how every day will examine, accuse, expose and condemn him; and how meekly he will accept the exposures and the condemnations! That man will not need you to preach to him about the sanctifying of the Sabbath, or about waiting on this and that means of grace. He will grow with or without the means of grace, but he will be of all men the most diligent in his devotion to them. He will almost get beyond the Word and within the Sacrament, so close up will his corruptions drive him to Christ and to God. Till, having provided for that man so much grace and so much growth in grace, God will soon have to give him glory, if only to satisfy him and pacify him and lift him out of the winter of his discontent. And then, 'Thy sun shall no more go down; neither shall thy moon withdraw herself; for the Lord shall be thine everlasting light, and the days of thy mourning shall be ended.'

---

# VII.  LADY BOYD

'Be sorry at corruption.'-- **Rutherford**.

Out of various published and unpublished writings of her day we are able to gather an interesting and impressive picture of Lady Boyd's life and character. But there was a carefully written volume of manuscript, that I much fear she must have burned when on her death-bed, that would have been invaluable to us to-night. Lady Boyd kept a careful diary for many years of her later life, and it was not a diary of court scandal or of social gossip or even of family affairs, it was a memoir of herself that would have satisfied even John Foster, for in it she tried with all fidelity to 'discriminate the successive states of her mind, and so to trace the progress of her character, a progress that gives its chief importance to human life.' Lady Boyd's diary would, to a certainty, have pleased the austere Essayist, for she was a woman after his own heart, 'grave, diligent, prudent, a rare pattern of Christianity.'

Thomas Hamilton, Lady Boyd's father, was an excellent scholar and a very able man. He rose from being a simple advocate at the Scottish Bar to be Lord President of the Court of Session, after which, for his great services, he was created Earl of Haddington. Christina, his eldest daughter, inherited no small part of her father's talents and strength of character. By the time we know her she has been some ten years a widow, and all her children are promising to turn out an honour to her name and a blessing to her old age. And, under the Divine promise, we do not wonder at that, when we see what sort of mother they had. For with all sovereign and inscrutable exceptions the rule surely still holds, 'Train up a child in the way he should go, and when he is old he will not depart from it.' All her days Lady Boyd was on the most intimate terms with the most eminent ministers of the Church of

Scotland. We find such men as Robert Bruce, Robert Blair, John Livingstone, and Samuel Rutherford continually referring to her in the loftiest terms. But it was not so much her high rank, or her great ability, or her fearless devotion to the Presbyterian and Evangelical cause that so drew those men around her; it was rather the inwardness and the intensity of her personal religion. You may be a determined upholder of a Church, of Presbytery against Prelacy, of Protestantism against Popery, or even of Evangelical religion against Erastianism and Moderatism, and yet know nothing of true religion in your own heart. But men like Livingstone and Rutherford would never have written of Lady Boyd as they did had she not been a rare pattern of inward and spiritual Christianity.

I have spoken of Lady Boyd's diary. 'She used every night,' says Livingstone, 'to write what had been the state of her soul all day, and what she had observed of the Lord's doing.' When all her neighbours were lying down without fear, her candle went not out till she had taken pen and ink and had called herself to a strict account for the past day. Her duties and her behaviour to her husband, to her children, to her servants, and to her many dependants; the things that had tried her temper, her humility, her patience, her power of self-denial; any strength and wisdom she had attained to in the government of her tongue and in shutting her ears from the hearing of evil; as, also, every ordinary as well as extraordinary providence that had visited her that day, and how she had been able to recognise it and accept it and take good out of it. Thus the Lady Boyd prevented the night-watches. When the women of her own rank sat down to write their promised letters of gossip and scandal and amusement she sat down to write her diary. 'We see many things, but we observe nothing,' said Rutherford in a letter to Lady Kenmure. All around her God had been dealing all that day with Lady Boyd's neighbours as well as with her, only they had not observed it. But she had not only an eye to see but a mind and a heart to observe also. She had a heart that, like the fabled Philosopher's Stone, turned all it touched and all that touched it immediately to fine gold. Riding home late one night from a hunting supper-party, young Lord Boyd saw his mother's candle still burning, and he made bold to knock at her door to ask why she was not asleep. Without saying a word, she took her son by the hand and set him down at her table and pointed him to the wet sheet she had just written. When he had read it he rose, without speaking a word, and went to his own room, and though that night was never all their days spoken of to one another, yet all his days Lord Boyd looked back on that night of the hunt as being the night when his soul escaped from the snare of the fowler. I much fear the diary is lost, but it would be well worth the trouble of the owner of Ardross Castle to cause a careful search to be made for it in the old charter chests of the family.

Till Lady Boyd's lost diary is recovered to us let us gather a few things about this remarkable woman out of the letters and reminiscences of such men as Livingstone and Rutherford and her namesake, Principal Boyd of Trochrig. Rutherford, especially, was, next to her midnight page, her ladyship's confidential and bosom friend. 'Now Madam,' he writes in a letter from Aberdeen, 'for your ladyship's own case.' And then he addresses himself in his finest style to console his correspondent, regarding some of the deepest and most painful incidents of her rare and genuine Christian experience. 'Yes,' he says, 'be sorry at corruption, and be not secure about yourself as long as any of it is there.' Corruption, in this connection, is a figure of speech. It is a kind of technical term much in vogue with spiritual writers of the profounder kind. It expresses to those unhappy persons who have the thing in themselves, and who are also familiar with the Scriptural and experimental use of the word--to them it expresses with fearful truth and power the sinfulness of their own hearts, as that sinfulness abides and breaks out continually. Now, how could Lady Boyd, being the woman she was, but be sorry and inconsolably sorry to find all that in her own heart every day? No wonder that she and her son never referred to what she had written and he had read in his mother's lockfast book that never-to-be-forgotten night.

'Be sorry at corruption, and be not secure.' How could she be secure when she saw and felt every day that deadly disease eating at her own heart? She could not be secure for an hour; she would have been anything but the grave and prudent woman she was--she would have been mad--had she for a single moment felt secure with such a corrupt heart. You must all have read a dreadful story that went the round of the newspapers the other day. A prairie hunter came upon a shanty near Winnipeg, and found--of all things in the world!--a human foot lying on the ground outside the door. Inside was a young English settler bleeding to death, and almost insane. He had lost himself in the prairie-blizzard till his feet were frozen to mortification, and in his desperation he had taken a carving-knife and had hacked

off his most corrupt foot and had thrown it out of doors. And then, while the terrified hunter was getting help, the despairing man cut off the other corrupt foot also.
I hope that brave young Englishman will live till some Winnipeg minister tells him
of a yet more terrible corruption than ever took hold of a frozen foot, and of a knife
that cuts far deeper than the shanty carver, and consoles him in death with the assurance that it was of him that Jesus Christ spoke in the Gospel long ago, when He
said that it is better to enter into life halt and maimed, rather than having two feet
to be cast into everlasting fire. There was no knife in Ardross Castle that would
reach down to Lady Boyd's corrupt heart; had there been, she would have first
cleansed her own heart with it, and would then have shown her son how to cleanse
his. But, as Rutherford says, she also had come now to that 'nick' in religion to cut
off a right hand and a right foot so as to keep Christ and the life everlasting, and so
had her eldest son, Lord Boyd. As Bishop Martensen also says, 'Many a time we
cannot avoid feeling a deep sorrow for ourselves because of the bottomless depth of
corruption which lies hidden in our heart--which sorrow, rightly felt and rightly
exercised, is a weighty basis of sanctification.'

To an able woman building on such a weighty basis as that on which Lady Boyd
had for long been building, Rutherford was quite safe to lay weighty and unusual
comforts on her mind and on her heart. 'Christ has a use for all your corruptions,'
he says to her, to her surprise and to her comfort. 'Beata culpa,' cried Augustine;
and 'Felix culpa,' cried Gregory. 'My sins have in a manner done me more good
than my graces,' said holy Mr. Fox. 'I find advantages of my sins,' said that most
spiritually-minded of men, James Fraser of Brea. Those who are willing and able
to read a splendid passage for themselves on this paradoxical- sounding subject will
find it on page xii. of the Address to the Godly and Judicious Reader in Samuel Rutherford's *Christ Dying and Drawing Sinners to Himself*.

What Rutherford was bold to say to Lady Boyd about her corruptions she was
able herself to say to Trochrig about her crosses. 'Right Honourable Sir,--It is common to God's children and to the wicked to be under crosses, but their crosses chase
God's children to God. O that anything would chase me to my God!' There speaks a
woman of mind and of heart who knows what she is speaking about. And, like her
and her correspondents, when all our other crosses have chased us to God, then our
master cross, the corruption of our heart, will chase us closer up to God than all our

other crosses taken together. We have no cross to be compared with our corruptions, and when they have chased us close enough and deep enough into the secret place of God, then we will begin to understand and adorn the dangerous doxologies of Augustine and Gregory, Fraser and Fox. Yes; anything and everything is good that chases us up to God: crosses and corruptions, sin and death and hell. 'O that anything would chase me to my God!' cried saintly Lady Boyd. And that leads her ladyship in another letter to Trochrig to tell him the kind of preaching she needs and that she must have at any cost. 'It will not neither be philosophy nor eloquence that will draw me from the broad road of perdition: I must have a trumpet to tell me of my sins.' That was a well-said word to the then Principal of Glasgow University who had so many of the future ministers of Scotland under his hands, all vying with one another as to who should be the best philosopher and the most eloquent preacher. Trochrig was both an eloquent preacher and a philosophic principal and a spiritually- minded man, but he was no worse to read Lady Boyd's demand for a true minister, and I hope he read her letter and gave his students her name in his pastoral theology class. 'Lady Boyd on the broad road of perdition!' some of his students would exclaim. 'Why, Lady Boyd is the most saintly woman in all the country.' And that would only give the learned Principal an opportunity to open up to his class, as he was so well fitted to do, that saying of Rutherford to Lady Kenmure: that 'sense of sin is a sib friend to a spiritual man,' till some, no doubt, went out of that class and preached, as Thomas Boston did, to 'terrify the godly.' Such results, no doubt, came to many from Lady Boyd's letter to the Principal as to the preaching she needed and must at any cost have: not philosophy, nor eloquence, but a voice like a trumpet to tell her of her sin.

Rutherford was in London attending the sittings of the Westminster Assembly when his dear friend Lady Boyd died in her daughter's house at Ardross. The whole Scottish Parliament, then sitting at St. Andrews, rose out of respect and attended her funeral. Rutherford could not be present, but he wrote a characteristically comforting letter to Lady Ardross, which has been preserved to us. He reminded her that all her mother's sorrows were comforted now, and all her corruptions healed, and all her much service of Christ and His Church in Scotland far more than recompensed.

Children of God, take comfort, for so it will soon be with you also. Your salvation, far off as it looks to you, is far nearer than when you believed. You will carry your corruptions with you to your grave; 'they lay with you,' as Rutherford said to Lady Boyd, 'in your mother's womb,' and the nearer you come to your grave the stronger and the more loathsome will you feel your corruptions to be; but what about that, if only they chase you the closer up to God, and make what is beyond the grave the more sure and the more sweet to your heart. Lady Boyd is not sorry for her corruptions now. She is now in that blessed land where the inhabitant shall not say, I am sick. Take comfort, O sure child of God, with the most corrupt heart in all the world; for it is for you and for the like of you that that inheritance is prepared and kept, that inheritance incorruptible, and undefiled, and that fadeth not away. Take comfort, for they that be whole need not a physician, but they that are sick.

# VIII. LADY ROBERTLAND

'That famous saint, the Lady Robertland, and the rare outgates she so
often got.'--Livingstone's *Characteristics*.

The Lady Robertland ranks in the Rutherford sisterhood with Lady Kenmure, Lady Culross, Lady Boyd, Lady Cardoness, Lady Earlston, Marion M'Naught and Grizel Fullarton. Lady Robertland, like so many of the other ladies of the Covenant, was not only a woman of deep personal piety and great patriotism, she was also, like Lady Kenmure, Lady Boyd, and Marion M'Naught, a woman of remarkable powers of mind. For one thing, she had a fascinating gift of conversation, and, like John Bunyan, it was her habit to speak of spiritual things with wonderful power under the similitude and parable of outward and worldly things. At the time of the famous 'Stewarton sickness' Lady Robertland was of immense service, both to the ministers and to the people. Robert Fleming tells us that the profane rabble of that time gave the nickname of the Stewarton sickness to that 'extraordinary outletting of the Spirit' that was experienced in those days over the whole of the west of Scotland, but which fell in perfect Pentecostal power on both sides of the Stewarton Water. 'I preached often to them in the time of the College vacation,' says Robert Blair, 'residing at the house of that famous saint, the Lady Robertland, and I had much conference with the people, and profited more by them than I think they did by me; though ignorant people and proud and secure livers called them "the daft people of Stewarton."' The Stewarton sickness was as like as possible, both in its manifestations and in its results, to the Irish Revival of 1859, in which, when it came over and awakened Scotland, the Duchess of Gordon, another lady of the Covenant, acted much the same part in the North that Lady Robertland acted in her day in the West. Many of our ministers still living can say of Huntly Lodge, 'I resided often there, and preached to the people, profiting more by them than they could have done by me.'

*Outgate* is an old and an almost obsolete word, but it is a word of great expressiveness and point. It bears on the face of it what it means. An outgate is just a *gate out*, a way of redemption, deliverance and escape. And her *rare* outgates does not imply that Lady Robertland's outgates were few, but that they were extraordinary, seldom matched, and above all expectation and praise. Lady Robertland's outgates were not rare in the sense of coming seldom and being few; for, the fact is, they filled her remarkable life full; but they were rare in the sense that she, like the Psalmist in Mr. James Guthrie's psalm, was a wonder unto many, and most of all unto herself. But a gate out, and especially such a gate as the Lady Robertland so often came out at, needs a key, needs many keys, and many keys of no common kind, and it needs a janitor also, or rather a redeemer and a deliverer of a kind corresponding to the kind of gate and the kind of confinement on which the gate shuts and opens. And when Lady Robertland thought of her rare outgates--and she thought more about them than about anything else that ever happened to her--and as often as she could get an ear and a heart into which to tell them, she always pictured to her audience and to herself the majestic Figure of the first chapter of the Revelation. She often spoke of her rare outgates to David Dickson, and Robert Blair, and John Livingstone, and to her own Stewarton minister, Mr. Castlelaw, whose name written in water on earth is written in letters of gold in heaven. 'Not much of a preacher himself, he encouraged his people to attend Mr. Dickson's sermons, and he often employed Mr. Blair to preach at Stewarton, and accompanied him back and forward, singing psalms all the way.' Her ladyship often told saintly Mr. Castlelaw of her rare outgates, and always so spoke to him of the Amen, who has the keys of hell and of death, that he never could read that chapter all his days without praising God that he had had the Lady Robertland and her rare outgates in his sin-sick parish.

But it is time to turn to some of those special and rare outgates that the Amen with the keys gave to His favoured handmaiden, the Lady Robertland; and the first kind of outgate, on account of which she was always such an astonishment to herself, was what she would call her outgate from providential disabilities, entanglements, and embarrassments. She was wont to say to William Guthrie, who best understood her witty words and her wonderful history, that the wicked fairies had handicapped her infant feet in her very cradle. She could use a freedom of speech with Guthrie, and he with her, such as neither of them could use with Livingstone or with Rutherford. Rutherford could not laugh when his heart was breaking, as Lady Robertland and the witty minister of Fenwick were often overheard laughing. 'Yes, but your Ladyship has won the race with all your weights,' Guthrie would laugh and say. 'One of my many races,' she would answer, with half a smile and half a sigh; 'but I have a long race, many long races, still before me. It seemed ***conclamatum est*** with me,' she would then say, quoting a well- known expression of Samuel Rutherford's, which is, being interpreted, It's all over and gone with me, 'but Providence, since the Amen took it in hand, has a thousand and more keys wherewith to give poor creatures like me our rare outgates.' There were few alive by that time who had known Lady Robertland in her early days, and she seldom spoke of those days; only, on the anniversary of her early marriage, she never forgot her feelings when her life as a Fleming came to an end and her new life as a Robertland began. There was a famous preacher of her day who sometimes spoke familiarly of the 'keys of the cupboard, that the Master carried at His girdle,' and she used sometimes to take up his homely words and say that she had had all the sweetest morsels and most delicate dainties of earth's cupboard taken out from under lock and key and put into her mouth. 'He ties terrible knots,' she would say, 'just to have the pleasure of loosing them off from those He loves. He lays nets and sets traps only that He may get a chance of healing broken bones and setting the terrified free.' No wonder that Wodrow calls her 'a much- exercised woman,' with such ingates and outgates, and with such miracles of an interposing Providence filling her childhood, her youth, her married and her widowed life. The ***Analecta*** is full of remarkable providences, but Lady Robertland's exercises and outgates are too wonderful even for the pages of that always wonderful and sometimes too awful book.

'My Master hath outgates of His own which are beyond the wisdom of man,' writes Rutherford, in her own language, to Lady Robertland from 'Christ's prison in Aberdeen.' Rutherford's letters are full of more or less mysterious allusions to the rare outgates that God in Christ had given him also from the snares and traps into which he had fallen by the sins and follies of his unregenerate youth. Whatever trouble came on Rutherford all his days--the persecution of the bishop, his banishment to Aberdeen, the shutting of his mouth from preaching Christ, the loss of wife and child, and the poignant pains of sanctification--he gathered them all up under the familiar figure of a waled and chosen cross. 'Seeing that the sins of my youth deserved strokes, how am I obliged to my Lord, who, out of many possible crosses, hath given me this waled and chosen cross to suffer for the name of Jesus Christ. Since I must have chains, He has put golden chains on me. Seeing I must have sorrow, for I have sinned, O Preserver of mankind, Thou hast waled and selected out for me a joyful sorrow--an honest, spiritual, glorious sorrow. Oh, what am I, such a rotten mass of sin, to be counted worthy of the most honourable rod in my Father's house, even the golden rod wherewith the Lord the Heir was Himself stricken. Thou wast a God that forgavest them, though Thou tookest vengeance of their inventions.' Rutherford also was forgiven, and the only vengeance that God took of his inventions, the irregularities of his youth, was taken in the form of a 'waled cross.' 'I might have been proclaimed on the crown of the causey,' says Rutherford, 'but He has so waled my cross and His vengeance that I am suffering not for my sin but for His name.' What a life hid with Christ in God he must live, who, like Rutherford, takes all his trials on earth as a transmuted and substituted cross for his sins: and who is able to take all his deserved and demanded chastisements in the shape of inward and spiritual and sanctifying pain. O sweet vengeance of grace on our sinful inventions! O most intimate and most awful of all our secrets, the secrets of a love-waled, love-substituted cross! O rare outgate from the scorn of the causeway to the smelting-house of 'Him who hath His fire in Zion!'

'The sorrows of death compassed me,' sings the Psalmist, and 'the pains of hell gat hold upon me; I found trouble and sorrow.' What, you may well ask, were those pains of hell that gat such hold of David while yet he was a living and unreprobated man? Was it not too strong language to use about any earthly experience, however terrible, to call it the pains of hell? Ask that man whose sin has found him out what he thinks the pains of hell were in David's case, and he will tell you that remorse--unsoftened, unsweetened, unquenchable remorse--is hell; at any rate, it is hell upon earth; and till he confessed his sin it was David's hell. Sin taken up and laid by God's hand on the sinner's conscience, that makes that sinner's conscience hell. And, then, do we not read that Jehovah laid on our Surety the sin of us all till He was three hours in hell for us, and came out of it, as Rutherford says, with the keys of hell at His proud girdle? And it is with those captured keys that He now unlocks the true hell-gate in every guilty sinner's conscience.

> 'He comes the prisoners to relieve
>   In Satan's bondage held;
> The gates of brass before Him burst,
>   The iron fetters yield.

. . . . . .

> We may not know, we cannot tell
>   What pains He had to bear,
> But we believe it was for us
>   He hung and suffered there.

> There was no other good enough
>   To pay the price of sin;
> He only could unlock the gate
>   Of heaven, and let us in.'

'Myself am hell,' cried out Satan, in his agony of pride and rage and remorse.

> 'Divines and dying men may talk of hell,
> But in my heart her several torments dwell.'

So you say of yourself, as you well may, after such a life as yours has been. The Judge of all the earth would not be a just judge unless hell were already kindled in your heart. But He who is a just God is also a Saviour, and He has with His own hand hung the key of hell and of your self-made bed in it at the girdle of Jesus Christ. Go to Him to-night, and tell Him that you are in hell. Tell Him that, like David, and very much, so far as you can understand, for David's sins, you, too, are in the pains of very hell. Cast yourself, like John in the Revelation, at His feet, and see if He does not say to you what He said through Nathan to David, and what He said Himself to John, and what He said to Lady Robertland, and what He said to Samuel

Rutherford. Cast yourself at His feet, and see if you do not get at His hands as rare an outgate and as wonderfully waled a cross as the very best of them got.

Then all the rest of your life on this prison-house of an earth will be a history in you and to you of all kinds of rare outgates. For, once He who has the keys has taken your case in hand, He will not let either rust or dust gather on His keys till He has opened every door for you and set you free from every snare. There are many evil affections, evil habits, and evil practices that are still closely padlocked both on your outward and your inward life that you must be wholly delivered from. And He who has all the keys of your body and your soul too at His girdle, will not consider that you have got your full outgate, or that He has at all discharged His duty by you, till, as Rutherford says, your sinful habits and practices are all loosened off from your life and are driven back into the inner world of your inclinations; and then, after that, He will only take up still more skilful and still more intricate keys wherewith to turn the locks of delight, desire, and inclination. O blessed keys of hell and of death, of habit and inclination and evil affection! O blessed people who are under such a Redeemer from sin and death and hell! O truly famous saint, the Lady Robertland, who got so many and so rare outgates from the Amen with the keys! Who shall give me an outgate from this body? cries the great apostle, not chafing in his chains for death, but for the true life that lies beyond death. Paul, with all his intense love of life and service--nay, because of that intense love--felt sometimes that this present life at its very best was but a life of relaxed imprisonment rather than of true liberty. Paul was, as we say, a kind of first-class misdemeanant, as Samuel Rutherford also was in his prison-palace in Aberdeen, and the Lady Robertland in Stewarton House; they had a liberty that was not to be despised; they had light and air and exercise; they were not in chains in the dungeon; they had pen and ink; they had books and papers, and their friends might on occasion visit them. They might have better food also if they paid for it; and, best of all, they could, till their full release came, beguile and occupy the time in work for Christ and His Church. But still they were present in this body of sin and death, and absent from the Lord, and they pined, and, I fear, sinfully murmured sometimes, for the last and the greatest and the best outgate of all. 'As for myself,' writes Rutherford, 'I think that if a poor, weak, dying sheep seeks for an old dyke, and the lee-side of a hill in a storm, I surely may be allowed to long for heaven. I see little in this life but sin, and the sour fruits of sin; and oh! what a burden and what a bitterness is sin!  What a miserable bondage it is to be at the nod of such a master as Sin!  But He who hath the keys hath sworn that our sin shall not loose the covenant bond, and therefore I wait in hope and in patience till His time shall come to take off all my fetters and make a hole in this cage of death that the imprisoned bird may find its long-promised liberty.'

'I would not live alway, thus fettered with sin,
Temptation without and corruption within;
In a moment of strength, if I sever the chain,
Scarce the victory is mine ere I'm captive again;
E'en the rapture of pardon is mingled with fears,
And the cup of thanksgiving with penitent tears;
The festival trump calls for jubilant songs,
But my spirit her own _miserere_ prolongs.

'Who, who would live always away from his God!
Away from yon heaven, that blissful abode
Where the rivers of pleasures flow o'er the bright plains,
And the noon-tide of glory eternally reigns;
Where the saints of all ages in harmony meet,
Their Saviour and brethren transported to greet;
While the songs of salvation exultingly roll,
And the love of the Lord is the bliss of the soul.'

# IX. JEAN BROWN

'Sin poisons all our enjoyments.'-- *Rutherford*.

Jean Brown was one of the selectest associates of the famous Rutherford circle. We do not know so much of Jean Brown outside of the Rutherford Letters as we would like to know, but her son, John Brown of Wamphray, is very well known to every student of the theology and ecclesiastical history of Scotland in the second half of the seventeenth century. 'I rejoice to hear about your son John. I had always a great love to dear John Brown. Remember my love to John Brown. I never could get my love off that man.' And all Rutherford's esteem and affection for Jean Brown's gifted and amiable son was fully justified in the subsequent history of the hard-working and well-persecuted parish minister of Wamphray. Letter 84 is a very remarkable piece of writing even in Rutherford, and the readers of this letter would gladly learn more than even its eloquent pages tell them about the woman who could draw such a letter out of Samuel Rutherford's mind and heart, the woman who was also the honoured mother of such a student and such a minister as John Brown of Wamphray. This letter has a *bite* in it--to use one of Rutherford's own words in the course of it--all its own. And it is just that profound and pungent element in this letter, that bite in it, that has led me to take this remarkable letter for my topic to-night.

There had been some sin in Samuel Rutherford's student days, or some stumble sufficiently of the nature of sin, to secretly poison the whole of his subsequent life. Sin is such a poisonous thing that even a mustard-seed of it planted in a man's youth will sometimes spring up into a thicket of terrible trouble both to himself and to many other people all his and all their days. An almost invisible drop of sin let fall into the wellhead of life will sometimes poison the whole broad stream of life, as well as all the houses and fields and gardens, with all their flowers and fruits, that are watered out of it. When any misfortune falls upon a Hebrew household, when any Jewish man or woman's sin finds them out, they say that there is an ounce of the golden calf on it. They open their Exodus and they read there in their bitterness of how Moses in his hot anger took the calf, which the children of Israel had polluted themselves with, and burned it in the fire, and ground it to powder, and strewed it upon the water, and made the children of Israel to drink of it. And, though God turned the poisoned, dust-laden waters of Samuel Rutherford's life into very milk and wine, yet to Rutherford's subtle and detective taste there was always a certain tang of the unclean and accursed thing in it. The best waled and most tenderly substituted cross in Rutherford's chastised life had always a certain galling corner in it that recalled to him, as he bled inwardly under it, the lack of complete purity and strict regularity in his youth. And it is to be feared that there are but too few men or women either who have not some Rutherford- like memory behind them that still clouds their now sheltered life and secretly poisons their good conscience. Some disingenuity, some simulation or dissimulation of affection, some downright or constructive dishonesty, some lack towards some one of open and entire integrity, some breach of good faith in spirit if not in letter, some still stinging tresspass of the golden rule, some horn or hoof of the golden calf, the bitter dust of which they taste to this day in their sweetest cup and at their most grace-spread table. There are more men and women in the Church of Christ than any one would believe who sing with a broken heart at every communion table: 'He hath not dealt with us after our sins, nor rewarded us according to our iniquities. As far as the east is from the west, so far hath He removed our transgressions from us.'

And even after such men and women might have learned a lesson, how soon we see all that lesson forgotten. Even after God's own hand has so conspicuously cut the bars of iron in sunder; after He has made the solitary to dwell in families; we still see sin continuing in new shapes and in other forms to poison the sweetest things in human life. What selfishness we see in family life, and that, too, after the vow and the intention of what self-suppression and self-denial. What impatience with one another, what bad temper, what cruel and cutting words, what coldness and rudeness and neglect, in how many ways our abiding sinfulness continues to poison the sweetest springs of life! And, then, how soon such unhappy men begin to see themselves reproduced and multiplied in their children. How many fathers see, with a secret bitterness of spirit that never can be told, their own worst vices of character and conduct reproduced and perpetuated in their children! One father sees his constitutional and unextirpated sensuality coming out in the gluttony, the drunkenness, and the lust of his son; while another sees his pride, his moroseness, his kept-up anger and his cruelty all coming out in one who is his very image. While many a mother sees her own youthful shallowness, frivolity, untruthfulness, deceit and parsimony in her daughter, for whose morality and religion she would willingly give up her own soul. And then our children, who were to be our staff and our crown, so early take their own so wilful and so unfilial way in life. They betake themselves, for no reason so much as just for intended disobedience and impudent independence, to other pursuits and pleasures, to other political and ecclesiastical parties than we have ever gone with. And when it is too late we see how we have again mishandled and mismanaged our families as we had mishandled and mismanaged our own youth, till it is only one grey head here and another there that does not go down to the grave under a crushing load of domestic sorrow. When the best things in life are so poisoned by sin, how bitter is that poison!

If an unpoisoned youth and an unembittered family life are some of the sweetest things this earth can taste, then a circle of close and true and dear friendships does not come very far behind them. Rutherford had plenty of trouble in his family life that he used to set down to the sins of his youth; and then the way he poisoned so many of his best friendships by his so poisonous party spirit is a humbling history to read. He quarrelled irreconcilably with his very best friends over matters that were soon to be as dead as Aaron's golden calf, and which never had much more life or decency in them. The matters were so small and miserable over which Rutherford quarrelled with such men as David Dickson and Robert Blair that I could not interest you in them at this time of day even if I tried. They were as parochial, as unsubstantial, and as much made up of prejudice and ill-will as were some of those matters that have served under Satan to poison so often our own private and public and religious life. Rutherford actually refused to assist Robert Blair at the Lord's Supper, so embittered and so black was his mind against his dearest friend. 'I would rather,' said sweet-tempered Robert Blair, 'have had my right hand hacked off at the cross of Edinburgh than have written such things.' 'My wife and I,' wrote dear

John Livingstone, 'have had more bitterness together over these matters than we have ever had since we knew what bitterness was.' And no one in that day had a deeper hand in spreading that bitterness than just the hand that wrote Rutherford's letters. There is no fear of our calling any man master if we once look facts fair in the face.

The precariousness of our best friendships, the brittle substance out of which they are all composed and constructed, and the daily accidents and injuries to which they are all exposed--all this is the daily distress of all true and loving hearts. What a little thing will sometimes embitter and poison what promised to be a loyal and lifelong friendship! A passing misunderstanding about some matter that will soon be as dead to us both as the Resolutions and Protestations of Rutherford's day now are to all men; an accidental oversight; our simple indolence in letting an absent friendship go too much out of repair for want of a call, or a written message, or a timeous gift: a thing that only a too-scrupulous mind would go the length of calling sin, will yet poison an old friendship and embitter it beyond all our power again to sweeten it. And, then, how party spirit poisons our best enjoyments as it did Rutherford's. How all our minds are poisoned against all the writers and the speakers, the statesmen and the journalists of the opposite camp, and even against the theologians and preachers of the opposite church. And, then, inside our own camp and church how new and still more malignant kinds of poison begin to distil out of our incurably wicked hearts to eat out the heart of our own nearest and dearest friendships. Envy, for one thing, which no preacher, not even Pascal or Newman, no moralist, no satirist, no cynic has yet dared to tell the half of the horrible truth about: drip, drip, drip, its hell-sprung venom soaks secretly into the oldest, the dearest and the truest friendship. Yes, let it be for once said, the viper-like venom of envy--the most loyal, the most honourable, the most self-forgetting and self-obliterating friendship is never in this life for one moment proof against it. We live by admiration; yes, but even where we admire our most and live our best this mildew still falls with its deadly damp. What did you suppose Rutherford meant when he wrote as he did write about himself and about herself to that so capable and so saintly woman, Jean Brown? Do you accuse Samuel Rutherford of unmeaning cant? Was he mouthing big Bible words without any meaning? Or, was he not drinking at that moment of the poison-filled cup of his own youthful, family, and friendship sins?  Nobody will persuade me that Rutherford was a canting hypocrite when he wrote those terrible and still unparaphrased words: 'Sin, sin, this body of sin and corruption embittereth and poisoneth all our enjoyments.  Oh that I were home where I shall sin no more!'

Puritan was an English nickname rather than a Scottish, but our Scots Presbyterians were Puritans at bottom like their English brethren both in their statesmanship and in their churchmanship, as well as in their family and personal religion.  And they held the same protest as the English Puritans held against the way in which the scandalous corruptions of the secular court, and the equally scandalous corruptions of the sacred bench, were together fast poisoning the public enjoyments of England and of Scotland.  You will hear cheap, shallow, vinous speeches at public dinners and suchlike resorts about the Puritans, and about how they denounced so much of the literature and the art of that day.  When, if those who so find fault had but the intelligence and the honesty to look an inch beneath the surface of things they would see that it was not the Puritans but their persecutors who really took away from the serious- minded people of Scotland and England both the dance and the drama, as well as so many far more important things in that day.  Had the Puritans and their fathers always had their own way, especially in England, those sources of public and private enjoyment would never have been poisoned to the people as they were and are, and that cleft would never have been cut between the conscience and some kinds of culture and delight which still exists for so many of the best of our people.  Charles Kingsley was no ascetic, and his famous *North British* article, 'Plays and Puritans,' was but a popular admission of what a free and religious-minded England owes on one side of their many-sided service to the Puritans of that impure day.  Christina Rossetti is no Calvinist, but she puts the Calvinistic and Puritan position about the sin-poisoned enjoyments of this life in her own beautiful way: 'Yes, all our life long we shall be bound to refrain our soul, and keep it low; but what then?  For the books we now forbear to read we shall one day be endued with wisdom and knowledge.  For the music we will not now listen to we shall join in the song of the redeemed.  For the pictures from which we turn we shall gaze unabashed on the beatific vision.  For the companionship we shun we shall be welcomed into angelic society and the companionship of triumphant saints.  For the amusements we avoid we shall keep the supreme jubilee. For all the pleasure we miss we shall abide, and for ever abide, in the rapture of heaven.'

All through Rutherford's lifetime preaching was his chiefest enjoyment and his most exquisite delight. He was a born preacher, and his enjoyment of preaching was correspondingly great. Even when he was removed from Anwoth to St. Andrews, where, what with his professorship and principalship together, one would have thought that he had his hands full enough, he yet stipulated with the Assembly that he should be allowed to preach regularly every Sabbath-day. But sin, again, that dreadful, and, to Rutherford, omnipresent evil, poisoned all his preaching also and made it one of the heaviest burdens of his conscience and his heart and his life. There is a proverb to the effect that when the best things become corrupt then that is corruption indeed. And so Rutherford discovered it to be in the matter of his preaching. Do what he would, Rutherford, like Shepard, could not keep the thought of what men would think out of his weak and evil mind, both before, and during, but more especially after his preaching. And that poisoned and corrupted and filled the pulpit with death to Rutherford, in a way and to a degree that nobody but a self-seeking preacher will believe or understand. Rutherford often wondered that he had not been eaten up of worms in his pulpit like King Herod on his throne, and that for the very same atheistical and blasphemous reason.

Those in this house who have followed all this with that intense and intelligent sympathy that a somewhat similar experience alone will give, will not be stumbled to read what Rutherford says in his letter to his near neighbour, William Glendinning: 'I see nothing in this life but sin, sin and the sour fruits of sin. O what a miserable bondage it is to be at the nod and beck of Sin!' Nor will they wonder to read in his letter to Lady Boyd, that she is to be sorry all her days on account of her inborn and abiding corruptions. Nor, again, that he himself was sick at his heart, and at the very yolk of his heart, at sin, dead-sick with hatred and disgust at sin, and correspondingly sick with love and longing after Jesus Christ. Nor, again, that he awoke ill every morning to discover that he had not yet awakened in his Saviour's sinless likeness. Nor will you wonder, again, at the seraphic flights of love and worship that Samuel Rutherford, who was so poisoned with sin, takes at the name and the thought of his divine Physician. For to Rutherford that divine Physician has promised to come 'the second time without sin unto salvation.' The first time He came He sucked the poison of sin out of the souls of sinners with His own lips, and out of all the enjoyments that He had sanctified and prepared for them in heaven. And He is coming back--He has now for a long time come back and taken Rutherford home to that sanctification that seemed to go further and further away from Rutherford the longer he lived in this sin-poisoned world. And, amongst all those who are now home in heaven, I cannot think there can be many who are enjoying heaven with a deeper joy than Samuel Rutherford's sheer, solid, uninterrupted, unadulterated, and unmitigated joy.

## X. JOHN GORDON OF CARDONESS, THE YOUNGER

'Put off a sin or a piece of a sin every day.'-- **Rutherford**.

If that gaunt old tower of Cardoness Castle could speak, and would tell us all that went on within its walls, what a treasure to us that story would be! Even the sighs and the meanings that visit us from among its mouldering stones tell us things that we shall not soon forget. They tell us how hard a task old John Gordon found salvation to be in that old house; and they tell us still, to deep sobs, how hard it was to him to see the sins and faults of his own youth back upon him again in the sins and faults of his son and heir. Old John Gordon's once so wild heart was now somewhat tamed by the trials of life, by the wisdom and the goodness of his saintly wife, and not least by his close acquaintance with Samuel Rutherford; but the comfort of all that was dashed from his lips by the life his eldest son was now living. Cardoness had always liked a good proverb, and there was a proverb in the Bible he often repeated to himself in those days as he went about his grounds: 'The fathers have eaten sour grapes, and the children's teeth are set on edge.' The miserable old man was up to the neck in debt to the Edinburgh lawyers; but he was fast discovering that there are other and worse things that a bad man entails on his eldest son than a burdened estate. There was no American wheat or Australian wool to reduce the rents of Cardoness in that day; but he had learnt, as he rode in to Edinburgh again and again to raise yet another loan for pocket-money to his eldest son, that there are far more fatal things to a small estate than the fluctuations and depressions of the corn and cattle markets. Gordon's own so expensive youth was now past, as he had hoped: but no, there it was, back upon him again in a most unlooked-for and bitter shape. 'The fathers have eaten sour grapes' was all he used to say as he rose to let in his drunken son at midnight; he scarcely blamed him; he could only blame himself, as his beloved boy reeled in and cursed his father, not knowing what he did.

The shrinking income of the small estate could ill afford to support two idle and expensive families, but when young Cardoness broke it to his mother that he wished to marry, she and her husband were only too glad to hear it. To meet the outlay connected with the marriage, and to provide an income for the new family, there was nothing for it but to raise the rents of the farms and cottages that stood on the estate. Anxious as Rutherford was to see young Cardoness settled in life, he could not stand by in silence and see honest and hard-working people saddled with the debts and expenses of the Castle; and he took repeated opportunities of telling the Castle people his mind; till old Cardoness in a passion chased him out of the house, and rode next Sabbath-day over to Kirkdale and worshipped in the parish church of William Dalgleish. The insolent young laird continued, at least during the time of his courtship, to go to church with his mother, but Rutherford could not shut his eyes to the fact that he studied all the time how he could best and most openly insult his minister. He used to come to church late on the Sabbath morning; and he never remained till the service was over, but would rise and stride out in his spurs in the noisiest way and at the most unseemly times. Rutherford's nest at Anwoth was not without its thorns. And that such a crop of thorns should spring up to him and to his people from Lady Cardoness's house, was one of Rutherford's sorest trials. The marriage- day, from which so much was expected, came and passed away; but what it did for young Cardoness may be judged from such expressions in Rutherford's Aberdeen letters as these: 'Be not rough with your wife. God hath given you a wife, love her; drink out of your own fountain, and sit at your own fireside. Make conscience of cherishing your wife.' His marriage did not sanctify young Cardoness; it did not even civilise him; for, long years after, when he was an officer in the Covenanters' army, he writes from Newcastle, apologising to his ill-used wife for the way he left her when he went to join his regiment: 'We are still ruffians and churls at home long after we are counted saints abroad.'

One day when Rutherford was in the Spirit in his silent prison, whether in the body or out of the body, he was caught up into Paradise to see the beauty of his Lord, and to hear his little daughter singing Glory. And among the thousands of children that sang around the throne he told young Cardoness that he saw and heard little Barbara Gordon, whose death had broken every heart in Cardoness Castle. 'I give you my word for it,' wrote Rutherford to her broken-hearted father, 'I saw two Anwoth children there, and one of them was your child and one of them was mine.' And when another little voice was silenced in the Castle to sing Glory in heaven, Rutherford could then write to young Cardoness all that was in his heart; he could not write too plainly now or too often. Not that you are to suppose that they were all saints now at Cardoness Castle, or that all their old and inherited vices of heart and character were rooted out: no number of deaths will do that to the best of us till our own death comes; but it was no little gain towards godliness when Rutherford could write to young Gordon, now old with sorrow, saying, 'Honoured and dear brother, I am refreshed with your letter, and I exhort you by the love of Christ to set to work upon your own soul. Read this to your wife, and tell her that I am witness for Barbara's glory in heaven.'

We would gladly shut the book here, and bring the Cardoness correspondence to a close, but that would not be true to the whole Cardoness history, nor profitable for ourselves. We have buried children, like John Gordon; and, like him, we have said that it was good for us to be sore afflicted; but not even the assurance that we have children in heaven has, all at once, set our affections there, or made us meet for entrance there. We feel it like a heavy blow on the heart, it makes us reel as if we had been struck in the face, to come upon a passage like this in a not-long-after letter to little Barbara Gordon's father: 'Ask yourself when next setting out to a night's drinking: What if my doom came to-night? What if I were given over to God's sergeants to-night, to the devil and to the second death?' And with the same post Rutherford wrote to William Dalgleish telling him that if young Cardoness came to see him he was to do his very best to direct and guide him in his new religious life. But Rutherford could not roll the care of young Cardoness over upon any other minister's shoulders; and thus it is that we have the long practical and powerful letter from which the text is taken: 'Put off a sin or a piece of a sin every day.'

Old Cardoness had been a passionate man all his days; he was an old man before he began to curb his passionate heart; and long after he was really a man of God, the devil easily carried him captive with his besetting sin. He bit his tongue till it bled as often as he recollected the shameful day when he swore at his minister in the rack-renting dispute. And he never rode past Kirkdale Church without sinning again as he plunged the rowels into his mare's unoffending sides. Cardoness did not read Dante, else he would have said to himself that his anger often filled his heart with hell's dunnest gloom. The old Castle was never well lighted; but, with a father and a son in it like Cardoness and his heir, it was sometimes like the Stygian pool itself. Rutherford had need to write to her ladyship to have a soft answer always ready between such a father and such a son. If you have the Inferno at hand, and will read what it says about the Fifth Circle, you will see what went on sometimes in that debt-drained and exasperated house. Rutherford was far away from Cardoness Castle, but he had memory enough and imagination enough to see what went on there as often as fresh provocation arose; and therefore he writes to young Gordon to put off a piece of his fiery anger every day. 'Let no complaining tenants, let no insulting letter, let no stupid or disobedient servant, let no sudden outburst of your father, let no peevish complaint of your wife make you angry. Remember every day that sudden and savage anger is one of your besetting sins: and watch against it, and put a piece of it off every day. Determine not to speak back to your father even if he is wrong and is doing a wrong to you and to your mother; your anger will not make matters better: hold your peace, till you can with decency leave the house, and go out to your horses and dogs till your heart is again quiet.'

Rutherford was not writing religious commonplaces when he wrote to Cardoness Castle; if he had, we would not have been reading his letters here to-night. He wrote with his eye and his heart set on his correspondents. And thus it is that 'night-drinking' occurs again and again in his letters to young Gordon. The Cardoness bill to Dumfries for drink was a heavy one; but it seems never to have occurred, even to the otherwise good people of those days, that strong drink was such a costly as well as such a dangerous luxury. It distresses and shocks us to read about 'midnight drinking' in Cardoness Castle, and in the houses round about, after all they had come through, but there it is, and we must not eviscerate Rutherford's outspoken letters. The time is not so far past yet with ourselves when we still went on drinking, though we were in debt for the necessaries of life, and though our sons reeled home from company we had made them early acquainted with. If you will not even yet pass the wine altogether, take a little less every day, and the good conscience it will give you will make up for the forbidden bouquet; till, as Rutherford said to Gordon, 'You will more easily master the remainder of your corruptions.'

Let us all try Samuel Rutherford's piecemeal way of reformation with our own anger; let us put a bridle on our mouths part of every day. Let us do this if we can as yet go no further; let us bridle our mouths on certain subjects, and about certain people, and in certain companies. If you have some one you dislike, some one who has injured or offended you, some rival or some enemy, whom to meet, to see, to read or to hear the name of, always brings hell's dunnest gloom into your heart-- well, put off this piece of your sin concerning him; do not speak about him. I do not say you can put the poison wholly out of your heart; you cannot: but you can and you must hold your peace about him. And if that beats you--if, instead of all that making you more easily master of your corruption, it helps you somewhat to discover how deep and how deadly it is--then Samuel Rutherford will not have written this old letter in vain for you.

## XI. ALEXANDER GORDON OF EARLSTON

'A man of great spirit, but much subdued by inward exercise.'
Livingstone's *Characteristics*.

The Gordons of Airds and Earlston could set their family seal to the truth of the promise that the mercy of the Lord is from everlasting to everlasting upon them that fear Him, and His righteousness to children's children. For the life of grace entered the Gordon house three long generations before it came to our Alexander of to-night, and it still descended upon his son and his son's son. His great-grandfather, Alexander Gordon also, was early nicknamed 'Strong Sandy,' on account of his gigantic size and his Samson-like strength. While yet a young man, happily for himself and for all his future children, as well as for the whole of Galloway, Gordon had occasion to cross the English border on some family business, to buy cattle or cutlery or what not, when he made a purchase he had not intended to make when he set out. He brought home with him a copy of Wycliffe's contraband New Testament, and from the day he bought that interdicted book till the day of his death, Strong Sandy Gordon never let his purchase out of his own hands. He carried his Wycliffe about with him wherever he went, to kirk and to market; he would as soon have thought of leaving his purse or his dirk behind him as his Wycliffe, his bosom friend. And many were the Sabbath-days that the laird of Earlston read his New Testament in the woods of Earlston to his tenants and neighbours, the Testament in the one hand and the dirk in the other. Tamed and softened as old Sandy Gordon became by that taming and softening book, yet there were times when the old Samson still came to the surface. As the Sabbath became more and more sanctified in Reformed Scotland, the Saints' days of the Romish Calendar fell more and more into open neglect, till the Romish clergy got an Act passed for the enforced observance of all the fasts and festivals of the Romish Communion. One of the enacted clauses forbade a plough to be yoked on Christmas Day, on pain of the forfeiture and public sale of the cattle that drew the plough. Old Earlston, at once to protest against the persecution, and at the same time to save his draught-oxen, yoked ten of his stalwart sons to the mid-winter plough, and, after ploughing the whole of Christmas Day, openly defied both priest and bishop to distrain his team. Christmas Day, whatever its claims and privileges might be, had no chance in Scotland till it came with better reasons than the threat of a Popish king and Parliament. The Patriarch of Galloway, as the south of Scotland combined to call old Alexander Gordon of Earlston, lived to the ripe age of over a hundred years, and we are told that he kept family worship himself to the day of his death, holding his Wycliffe in his own hand, and yielding it and his place at the family altar over to none.

But it is with the name-son and great-grandson of this sturdy old saint that we have chiefly to do to-night. And I may say of him, to begin with, that he was altogether worthy to inherit and to hand on the tradition of family grace and truth that had begun so early and so conspicuously with the head of the Earlston house. 'Alexander Gordon of Earlston,' says John Livingstone, in one of his priceless little etchings, 'was a man of great spirit, but much subdued by inward exercise, and who attained the most rare experiences of downcasting and uplifting.' And in Rutherford's first letter to this Earlston, written from Anwoth in 1636, he says, in that lofty oracular way of his, 'Jesus Christ has said that Alexander Gordon must lead the ring in Galloway in witnessing a good conscience.' This, no doubt, refers to the prosecution that Gordon was at that moment undergoing at the hands of the Bishop of Glasgow for refusing to admit a nominee of the Bishop into the pulpit of a reclaiming parish. It would have gone still worse with Earlston than it did had not Lord Lorne, the true patron of the parish, taken his place beside Earlston at the Bishop's bar, and testified his entire approval of all that Earlston had done. With all that, the case did not end till Earlston was banished beyond the Tay for his resistance to the will of the Bishop of Glasgow. This all took place in the early half of the seventeenth century, so that Dr. Robert Buchanan might with more correctness have entitled his able book 'The Two Hundred Years' Conflict' than 'The Ten,' so early was the battle for Non-Intrusion begun in Galloway. Alexander Gordon was a Free

Churchman 200 years before the Disruption, and Lord Lorne was the forerunner of those evangelical and constitutional noblemen and gentlemen in Scotland who helped so much to carry through the Disruption of 1843. We find both Lord Lorne, and Earlston his factor, sitting as elders beside one another in the Glasgow Assembly of 1638, and then we find Earlston the member for Galloway in the Parliament of 1641.

We do not know exactly on what occasion it was that Earlston refused to accept the knighthood that was offered him by the Crown; but we seem to hear the old Wycliffite come back again in his great-grandson as he said, 'No, your Majesty, excuse and pardon me; but no.' Alexander Gordon felt that it would be an everlasting dishonour to him and to his house to let his shoulder be touched in knighthood by a sword that was wet, and that would soon be still more wet, with the best blood in Scotland. 'No, your Majesty, no.'

Almost all that we are told about Earlston in the histories of his time bears out the greatness of his spirit; that, and the stories that gives rise to, take the eye of the ordinary historian; but good John Livingstone, though not a great historian in other respects, is by far the best historian of that day for our purpose. John Livingstone's *Characteristics* is a perfect gallery of spiritual portraits, and the two or three strokes he gives to Alexander Gordon make him stand out impressively and memorably to all who understand and care for the things of the Spirit.

'A man of great spirit, but much subdued by inward exercise.' I do not need to tell you what exercise is--at least bodily exercise. All that a man does to draw out, develop, and healthfully occupy his bodily powers in walking, riding, running, wrestling, carrying burdens, and leaping over obstacles--all that is called bodily exercise, and some part of that is absolutely necessary every day for the health of the body and for the continuance and the increase of its strength. But we are not all body; we are soul as well, and much more soul than body. Bodily exercise profiteth little, says the Apostle,--compared, that is, with the exercise of the soul, of the mind, and of the heart. Now, Alexander Gordon was such an athlete of the heart that all who knew him saw well what exercise he must have gone through before he was subdued in his high mind and proud spirit to be so humble, so meek, so silent, so unselfish, and so full of godliness and brotherly kindness--what a world of inward exercise all that bespoke! Alexander Gordon's patience under wrong, his low esteem of himself and of all he did, his miraculous power over himself in the forgiveness of enemies and in the forgetfulness of injuries, his contentment amid losses and disappointments, his silence when other men were bursting to speak, and his openness to be told that when he did speak he had spoken rashly, unadvisedly, and offensively--in all that Earlston was a conspicuous example of what inward exercise carried on with sufficient depth and through a sufficiently long life will do even for a man of a hot temper and a proud heart. Alexander Gordon had, to begin with, a large heart. A large heart was a family possession of the Gordons; the fathers had it and the mothers had it; and whatever came and went in the family estate, the Gordon heart was always entailed unimpaired--increased indeed--upon the children. And after some generations of true religion, inwardly and deeply exercising the Gordon heart, it almost came as a second nature to our Gordon to take to heart all that happened to him, and to exercise his large and deep heart yet more thoroughly with it. The affairs of the family, the affairs of the estate, the affairs of the Church, his duties as a landlord, a farmer, a heritor, and a factor, and the persecutions and sufferings that all these things brought upon him, some of which we know--all that found its way into Earlston's wide and deep and still unsanctified heart. And then, there is a law and a provision in the life of grace that all those men come to discover who live before God as Earlston lived, a provision that secures to such men's souls a depth, and an inwardness, and an increasing exercise that carries them on to reaches of inward sanctification that the ruck and run of so-called Christians know nothing about, and are incapable of knowing.

Such men as Earlston, while the daily rush of outward things is let in deeply into their hearts, are not restricted to these things for the fulness of their inward exercise; their own hearts, though there were no outward world at all, would sufficiently exercise them to all the gifts and graces and attainments of the profoundest spiritual life. For one thing, when once Earlston had begun to keep watch over his own heart in the matter of its motives--it was David Dickson, one fast-day at Irvine, on 1 Sam. ii., who first taught Gordon to watch his motives--from that day Rutherford and Livingstone, and all his family, and all his fellow- elders saw a change in their friend that almost frightened them. There was after that such a far-off tone in his letters, and such a far-off look in his eyes, and such a far-off sound in his voice as they all felt must have come from some great, and, to them, mysterious advance in his spiritual life; but he never told even his son William what it was that had of late so softened and quieted his proud and stormy heart. But, all the time, it was his motives. The baseness of his motives even when he did what it was but his duty and his praise to do, that quite killed Earlston every day. The loathsomeness of a heart that hid such motives in its unguessed depths made him often weep in the woods which his grandfather had sanctified by his Bible readings a century before. Rutherford saw with the glance of genius what was going on in his friend's heart, when, in one letter, not referring to himself at all, Earlston suddenly said, 'If Lucifer himself would but look deep enough and long enough into his own heart, the sight of it would make him a little child.' 'Did not I say,' burst out Rutherford, as he read, 'that Alexander Gordon would lead the ring in Galloway?'

Earlston frightened into silence the Presbytery of Kirkcudbright on one occasion also, when at their first meeting after he had spoken out so bravely before the king and the Parliament, and they were to move him a vote of thanks, he cried out: 'Fathers and brethren, the heart is deceitful above all things, and desperately wicked, and you do not know it. For I had a deep, malicious, revengeful motive in my heart behind all my fine and patriotic speeches in Parliament. I hated Montrose more than I loved the freedom of the Kirk. Spare me, therefore, the sentence of putting that act of shame on your books!' It was discoveries like this that accumulated in John Livingstone's note-book till he blotted out all his instances and left only the blessed result, 'Alexander Gordon, a man of great spirit, but much subdued by inward exercise, and who was visited with most rare experiences of downcasting and uplifting.' No doubt, dear John Livingstone; we can well believe it. Too rare with us, alas! but every day with your noble friend; every day and every night, when he lay down and when he rose up. His very dreams often cast him down all day after them; for he said, If my heart were not one of the chambers of hell itself, such hateful things would not stalk about in it when the watchman is asleep. Downcastings! downcastings! Yes, down to such depths of self-discovery and self-detestation and self-despair as compelled his Heavenly Master to give commandment that His prostrate servant should be lifted up as few men on the earth have ever been lifted up, or could bear to be. Yes; they were rare experiences both of downcastings and of upliftings; when such downcastings and upliftings become common the end of this world will have come, and with it the very Kingdom of Heaven.

The last sight we see of Alexander Gordon in this world is after his Master has given commandment that the last touch be put to His servant's subdued and child-like humility. The old saint is sitting in his grandfather's chair and his wife is feeding him like a weaned child. John Livingstone tells that Mr. John Smith, a minister in Teviotdale, had all the Psalms of David by heart, and that instead of a curtailed, monotonous, and mechanical grace before meat he always repeated a whole Psalm. Earlston must have remembered once dining in the Manse of Maxton at a Communion time; for, as his tender-handed wife took her place beside his chair to feed her helpless husband, he always lifted up his palsied hand and always said to himself, to her, and above all, to God, the 131st Psalm--

'As child of mother weaned; my soul
Is like a weaned child;'

till all the godly households in Galloway knew the 131st Psalm as Alexander Gordon of Earlston's grace before meat.

## XII.  EARLSTON THE YOUNGER

'A renowned Gordon, a patriot, a good Christian, a confessor, and, I
may add, a martyr of Jesus Christ.'--Livingstone's ***Characteristics***.

Thomas Boston in his most interesting autobiography tells us about one of his elders who, though a poor man, had always 'a brow for a good cause.' Now nothing could better describe the Gordons of Earlston than just that saying.  For old Alexander Gordon, the founder of the family, lifted up his brow for the cause of the Bible and the Sabbath-day when his brow was as yet alone in the whole of Galloway; his great-grandson Alexander also lifted up his brow in his day for the liberty of public worship and the freedom of the courts and congregations of the Church of Scotland, and paid heavily for his courage; and his son William, of whom we are to speak to-night, showed the same brow to the end.  The Gordons, as John Howie says, have all along made no small figure in our best Scottish history, and that because they had always a brow for the best causes of their respective days.  As Rutherford also says, the truth kept the causey in the south-west of Scotland largely through the intelligence, the courage, and the true piety of the Gordon house.

While still living at home and assisting his father in his farms and factorships, young Earlston was already one of Rutherford's most intimate correspondents.  In a kind of reflex way we see what kind of head and heart and character young Earlston must already have had from the letters that Rutherford wrote to him.  If we are to judge of the character and attainments and intelligence of Rutherford's correspondents by the letters he wrote to them, then I should say that William Gordon of Earlston must have been a remarkable man very early in life, both in the understanding and the experience of divine things.  One of the Aberdeen letters especially, numbered 181 in Dr. Andrew Bonar's edition, for intellectual power, inwardness, and eloquence stands almost if not altogether at the head of all the 365 letters we have from Rutherford's pen. He never wrote an abler or a better letter than that he wrote to William Gordon the younger of Earlston on the 16th of June 1637. Not James Durham, not George Gillespie, not David Dickson themselves ever got a stronger, deeper, or more eloquent letter from Samuel Rutherford than did young William Gordon of Airds and Earlston. William Gordon was but a young country laird, taken up twelve hours every day and six days every week with fences and farm-houses, with horses and cattle, but I think an examination paper on personal religion could be set out of Rutherford's letters to him that would stagger the candidates and the doctors of divinity for this year of grace 1891. 'William Gordon was a gentlemen,' says John Howie, 'of good parts and endowments; a man devoted to religion and godliness.' Unfortunately we do not possess any of the letters young Earlston wrote to Rutherford. I wish we did. I would have liked to have seen that letter of Gordon's that so 'refreshed' Rutherford's soul; and that other letter of which Rutherford says that Gordon will be sure to 'come speed' with Christ if he writes to heaven as well about his troubles as he had written to Rutherford in Aberdeen. What a detestable time that was in Scotland when such a man as William Gordon was fined, and fined, and fined; hunted out of his house and banished, till at last he was shot by the soldiers of the Crown and thrown into a ditch as if he had been a highwayman.

The first thing that strikes me in reading Rutherford's letters to young Earlston and to several other young men of that day is the extraordinary frankness and self-forgetfulness of the writer. He takes his young correspondents into his confidence in a remarkable way. He opens up his whole heart to them. He goes back with a startling boldness and unreserve and plainness of speech on his own youth, and he lays himself alongside of his youthful correspondents in a way that only a strong man and a humble could afford to do. Let young men read Rutherford's letters to young William Gordon of Earlston, and to young John Gordon of Cardoness, and to young Lord Boyd, and such like, and they will be surprised to find that even Samuel Rutherford was once a young man exactly like themselves, and that he never forgot the days of his youth nor the trials and temptations and transgressions of those perilous days. Let them read his Letters, and they will see that Rutherford could not only write home to the deepest experiences of Lady Boyd and Lady Kenmure and Marion M'Naught, but that he was quite as much at home with their sons and daughters also.

Rutherford told young Earlston how terribly he had 'ravelled his own hesp' in the days of his youth, and he tells another of his correspondents that after eighteen years he was not sure he had even yet got his ravelled hesp put wholly right. Young Edinburgh gentlemen who have been born with the silver spoon in their mouth will not understand what a ravelled hesp is. But those who have been brought up at the pirn- wheel in Thrums, and in suchlike handloom towns, have the advantage of some of their fellow-worshippers to-night. They do not need to turn to Dr. Bonar's Glossary or to Jamieson's Scottish Dictionary to find out what a ravelled hesp is. They well remember the stern yoke of their youth when they were sent supperless to bed because they had ravelled their hesp, and all the old times rush back on them as Rutherford confesses to Earlston how recklessly he ravelled his hesp when he was a student in Edinburgh, and how, twenty times a day, he still ravels it after he is Christ's prisoner in Aberdeen.

When the hesp is ravelled the pirn is badly filled, and then the shuttle is choked and arrested in the middle of its flight, the web is broken and knotted and uneven, and the weaver is dismissed, or, at best, he is fined in half his wages. And so, said Rutherford, is it with the weaver and the web of life, when a man's life-hesp is ravelled in the morning of his days. I stood not long ago at the grave's mouth of a dear and intimate friend of mine who had fatally ravelled both his own hesp and that of other people, till we had to get the grave-diggers to take a cord and help us to bury him. Horace said that in his day most men fled the empty cask; and all but two or three fled my poor friend's ravelled hesp. He had recovered the lost thread before he died, but his tangled life was past unravelling in this world, and we wrapped his ragged hesp around him for a winding-sheet, and left him with Christ, who so graciously took the cumber of Rutherford's ill-ravelled life also. Young men whose hesp still runs even, and whose web is not yet torn, as Rutherford says to Earlston, 'Make conscience of your thoughts and study in everything to mortify your lusts. Wash your hands in innocency, and God, who knoweth what you have need of before you ask Him, will Himself lead you to encompass His holy altar, and thus to enter the harbour of a holy home and an unravelled life.'

Rutherford's Letters are all gleaming with illustrations, some homely enough, like the ill-ravelled hesp, and some classically beautiful, like the arrow that has gone beyond the bowman's mastery. Writing to young Lord Boyd about seeking Christ in youth, and about the manifold advantages of an early and a complete conversion, Rutherford says: 'It is easy to set an arrow right before the string is drawn, but when once the arrow is in the air the bowman has lost all power over it.' Look around at the men and women beside you and see how true that is. Look at those whose arrow is shot, and see how impossible it is for them, even when they wish it, either to call their arrow back or to correct its erring flight. And thank God that you are still in your youth, and that the arrow of your future life is not yet shot. And while your arrow still lies trembling on the string be sure your face is in the right direction and your aim well taken. Rutherford, with all his experience and all his frankness and all his eloquence, could not tell his young correspondents half the advantages of an early conversion. Nor can I tell you half of the changes for good that would immediately take place in you with an early, immediate, and complete conversion. Perhaps the very first thing some of you would do would be to get a new minister and to join a new church. Then on the week-day some of you would at once leave your present business, and seek a new means of livelihood in which you could at least keep your hands and your conscience clean. Then you would choose a new friend and a new lover, or else you would get God to do for them what He has been so good as to do for you, give them a new heart with which to weave their hesp and shoot their arrow. You would read new books and new journals, or, else, you would read the old books and the old journals in a new way. The Sabbath-day would become a new day to you, the Bible a new book, and your whole future a new outlook to you;--but why particularise and specify, when all old things would pass away, and all things would become new? Oh dear young men of Edinburgh, and young men come up to Edinburgh to get your bow well strung and your arrow well winged, look well before you let go the string, for, once your arrow is shot, you cannot recall it so as to take a second aim. With an early and a complete conversion you would have the advantage also of having your whole life for growth in grace and for the knowledge of yourself, of the word of God and of Jesus Christ; for the formation of your character also, and for the service of God and of your generation. And then when your friends met around your grave, instead of hiding you and your ravelled hesp away in shame and silence, they would stand, a worshipping crowd, saying over you: 'Those that be planted in the house of the Lord shall flourish in the courts of our God. They shall still bring forth fruit in old age, they shall be fat and flourishing.'

And then, like the true and sure guide to heaven that Rutherford was, he led his young correspondents on from strength to strength, and from one degree and one depth of grace to another, as thus, 'Common honesty will not take a man to heaven. Many are beguiled with this, that they are clear of scandalous sins. But the man that is not born again cannot enter the Kingdom of Heaven. The righteous are scarcely saved. God save me from a disappointment, and send me salvation. Speer at Christ the way to heaven, for salvation is not soon found; many miss it. Say, I must be saved, cost me what it will.' And to a nameless young man, supposed to be one of his Anwoth parishioners, he writes, 'So my real advice is that you acquaint yourself with prayer, and with searching the Scriptures of God, so that He may shew you the only true way that will bring rest to your soul. Ordinary faith and country holiness will not save you. Take to heart in time the weight and worth of an immortal soul; think of death, and of judgment at the back of death, that you may be saved.--Your sometime pastor, and still friend in God, S. R.' The civility of the New Jerusalem, he is continually reminding his genteel and correct-living correspondents, is a very different thing from the civility of Edinburgh, or Aberdeen, or St. Andrews. And so it is, else it would not be worth both Christ and all Christian men both living and dying for it.

And this leads Rutherford on, in the last place, to say what Earlston, and Cardoness, and Lord Boyd, while yet in their unconversion and their early conversion, would not understand. For, writing to Robert Stuart, the son of the Provost of Ayr, Rutherford says to him, 'Labour constantly for a sound and lively sense of sin,' and to the Laird of Cally, 'Take pains with your salvation, for without much wrestling and sweating it is not to be won.' A sound and lively sense of sin. As we read these sound and lively letters, we come to see and understand something of what their writer means by that. He means that Stuart and Cally, Cardoness and Earlston, young laymen as they were, were to labour in sin and in their own hearts till they came to see something of the ungodliness of sin, something of its fiendishness, its malignity, its loathesomeness, its hell-deservingness, its hell-alreadyness. 'All his religious illuminations, affections, and comforts,' says Jonathan Edwards of David Brainerd, 'were attended with evangelical humiliation, that is to say, with a deep sense of his own despicableness and odiousness, his ignorance, pride, vileness, and pollution. He looked on himself as the least and the meanest of all saints, yea, very often as the vilest and worst of mankind.' But let Rutherford and Brainerd and Edwards pour out their blackest vocabulary upon sin, and still sin goes and will go without its proper name. Only let those Christian noblemen and gentlemen to whom Rutherford wrote, labour in their own hearts all their days for some sound and lively and piercing sense of this unspeakably evil thing, and they will know, as Rutherford wrote to William Gordon, that they have got to some sound and lively sense of sin when they feel that there is no one on earth or in hell that has such a sinful heart as they have. The nearer to heaven you get, the nearer will you feel to hell, said Rutherford to young Earlston, till, all at once, the door will open over you, and, or ever you are aware, you will be for ever with Christ and the blessed; as it indeed was with William Gordon at the end. For as he was on his way to join the Covenanters at Bothwell Bridge, he was shot by a gang of English dragoons and flung into a ditch. Jesus Christ, says Rutherford, went suddenly home to His father's house all over with his own blood, and it was surely enough for William Gordon that he went home like his Master.

# XIII.  ROBERT GORDON OF KNOCKBREX

'A single-hearted and painful Christian, much employed in parliaments and public meetings after the year 1638.'-- *Livingstone*.

'Hall-binks are slippery.'-- *Gordon to Rutherford*.

Robert Gordon of Knockbrex, in his religious character, was a combination of Old Honest and Mr. Fearing in the *Pilgrim's Progress*.  He was as single-hearted and straightforward as that worthy old gentleman was who early trysted one Good-Conscience to meet him and give him his hand over the river which has no bridge; and he was at the same time as troublesome to Samuel Rutherford, his minister and correspondent, as Greatheart's most troublesome pilgrim was to him.  In two well-chosen words John Livingstone tells us the deep impression that the laird of Knockbrex made on the men of his day.  With a quite Scriptural insight and terseness of expression, Livingstone simply says that Robert Gordon was the most 'single-hearted and painful' of all the Christian men known to his widely- acquainted and clear-sighted biographer.

Now there may possibly be some need that the epithet 'painful' should be explained, as it is here applied to this good man, but everybody knows without any explanation what it is for any man to be 'single-hearted.'  This was the fine character our Lord gave to Nathanael when He saluted him as an Israelite indeed in whom was no guile.  It is singleness of heart that so clears up the understanding and the judgment that, as our Lord said at another time, it fills a man's whole soul with light.  And Paul gives it as the best character that a servant can bring to or carry away from his master's house, that he is single-hearted and not an eye- servant in all that he says and does.  I keep near me on my desk a book called Roget's *Thesaurus*, which is a rich treasure-house of the English language. And though I thought I knew what Livingstone meant when he called Robert Gordon a single-hearted man, at the same time I felt sure that Roget would help me to see Gordon better. And so he did. For when I had opened his book at the word 'single-hearted,' he at once told me that Knockbrex was an open, frank, natural, straightforward, altogether trustworthy man. He was above-board, outspoken, downright, blunt even, and bald, always calling a spade a spade. And with each new synonym Robert Gordon's honest portrait stood out clearer and clearer before me, till I thought I saw him, and wished much that we had more single-hearted men like him in the public and the private life of our day.

And then, as to his 'painfulness,' we have that so well expounded and illustrated in John Bunyan's Mr. Fearing, that all I need to do is to recall that inimitable character to your happy memory. 'He was a man that had the root of the matter in him, but at the same time he was the most troublesome pilgrim that ever I met with in all my days. He lay roaring at the Slough of Despond for above a month together. He would not go back neither. The Celestial City, he said he should die if he came not to it, and yet was dejected at every difficulty and stumbled at every straw. He had, I think, a Slough of Despond in his mind, a slough that he carried everywhere with him, or else he could never have been as he was.' Yes, both Mr. Fearing and the laird of Knockbrex were painful Christians. That is to say, they took pains, special and exceptional pains, with the salvation of their own souls. They took their religion with tremendous earnestness. They would have pleased Paul had they lived in his day, for they both worked out their own salvation with fear and trembling. They looked on sin and death and hell with absorbing and overwhelming solemnity, and they set themselves with all their might to escape from these direst of evils. Pardon of sin, peace with God, a clean heart and a Christian character, all these things were their daily prayer; for these things they wrestled many a night like Jacob at the Jabbok. The day of death, the day of judgment, heaven and hell--these things were more present with them than the things they saw and handled every day. And this was why they were such troublesome pilgrims. This was why they sometimes stumbled at what their neighbours called a straw; and this was why they feared neither king nor bishop, man nor devil, they feared God and sin and death and hell so much. This was why, while all other men were so full of torpid assurance, they still carried, to the annoyance and anger of all their serene-minded neighbours, such a Slough of Despond in their anxious minds. This was why sin so poisoned all their possessions and enjoyments that Greatheart could not get Fearing, any more than Rutherford could get Gordon, out of the Valley of Humiliation. And this was why Gordon so often turned upon Rutherford when he was exalted above measure, and reminded his minister, in the old Scottish proverb, that 'Hall-binks are slippery.' Seats of honour, Mr. Samuel, are unsafe seats for unsanctified sinners. Ecstasies do not last, and they leave the soul weaker and darker than they found it. It is a comely thing even for a saint to be well-clothed about with humility, and the deepest valley is safer and seemlier walking for a lame man than the mountain-top; and so on, till Rutherford admitted that Robert Gordon's warnings were neither impertinent nor untimeous. The sin- stricken laird of Knockbrex was like Mr. Fearing at the House Beautiful. When all the other pilgrims sat down without fear at the table, that so timid and so troublesome pilgrim, remembering the proverb, stole away behind the screen and found his meat and his drink in overhearing the good conversation that went on in the banquet-hall. Gordon could not understand all Rutherford's joy. He did not altogether like it. He did not answer the ecstatic letters so promptly as he answered those which were composed on a soberer key. He was a blunt, plain-spoken, matter-of- fact man; he immensely loved and honoured his minister, but he could not help reminding him after one of his specially enraptured letters that 'Hall-binks are slippery seats.' The golden mean lay somewhere between the hall-bink and the ash-pit; somewhere between Rutherford's ecstasy and Gordon's depression. But as the Guide said in the exquisite conversation, the wise God will have it so, some must pipe and some must weep: and, for my part, I care not for that profession that begins not with heaviness of mind. Only, here was the imperfection of Mr. Fearing and Robert Gordon, that they would play upon no other music but this to their latter end. So much so, that the thick woods of Knockbrex are said to give out to this day the sound of the sackbut to those who have their ears set to such music; there are men in that country who say that they still hear it when they pass the plantations of Knockbrex alone at night. Knockbrex is now a fine modern mansion that is sometimes let for the summer to city people seeking solitude and rest. Among these thick woods and along these silent sands Samuel Rutherford and Robert Gordon were wont to walk and talk together. And here still a man who wishes it may be free from the noise and the hurrying of this life. Here a man shall not be let and hindered in his contemplations as in other places he is apt to be. There are woods here that he who loves a pilgrim's life may safely walk in. The soil also all hereabouts is rich and fruitful, and, under good management, it brings forth by handfuls. The very shepherd boys here live a merry life, and wear more of the herb called heart's- ease in their bosoms than he that is clad in silk and velvet. What a rich inheritance to the right heir is the old estate of Knockbrex! What an opportunity, and what an education, it must be to tenant Knockbrex with recollection, with understanding, and with sympathy even for a season.

Robert Gordon would very willingly have remained behind the screen all his days. He would very willingly have given himself up to the care of his estate, to the upbringing of his children, and to the working out of his own salvation, but such a man as he now was could not be hid. The stone that is fit for the wall is not let lie in the ditch. We have a valuable letter of Rutherford's addressed to Marion M'Naught about the impending election of a commissioner for Parliament for the town of Kirkcudbright. In that letter he urges her to try to get her husband, William Ful-larton, to stand for the vacant seat. 'It is an honourable and necessary service,' he says. And speaking of one of the candidates, he further says: 'I fear he has neither the skill nor the authority for the post.' Now, it was either at this election, or it was at the next election, that an influential deputation of the gentry and burgesses and ministers and elders of the district waited on Robert Gordon to get him to stand for one of the vacant seats in Galloway; and once he was chosen and had shown himself to the world he was never let return again to his home occupations. 'He was much employed in those years,' says Livingstone, 'in parliaments and public meetings.'

There are some good men among us who think that the world is so bad that it is fit for nothing but to be abandoned to the devil and his angels altogether, and that a genuine man of God is too good to be made a member of Parliament or to be much seen on the platforms of public meetings. Such was not Samuel Rutherford's judgment, as will be seen in his 36th Letter. And such was not Robert Gordon's judgment, when he left the woods and fields of Knockbrex and gave himself wholly up to the politics of his entangled and distressful day. What he would have said to the summons had the marches been already redd between Lex and Rex, and had the affairs of the Church of Christ not been still too much mixed up with the affairs of

the State, I do not know. Only, as long as the Crown and the Parliament had their
hands so deeply in the things of the Church, Knockbrex was not hard to persuade
to go to Parliament to watch over interests that were dearer to him than life, or
family, or estate. Robert Gordon carried the old family brow with him into all the
debates and dangers of that day; and he added to all that a singleness of heart and a
painstaking mind all his own. And it was no wonder that such a man was much in
demand at such a time. In our own far happier time what a mark does a member of
Parliament still make, or a speaker at public meetings, who is seen to be single in his
heart, and is at constant pains with himself and with all his duties. It is at bottom
our doubleness of heart and our lack of sufficient pains with ourselves and with the
things of truth and righteousness that so divide us up into bitter factions, hateful
and hating one another. And when all our public men are like Robert Gordon in
the singleness of their aims and their motives, and when they are at their utmost
pains to get at the truth about all the subjects they are called to deal with, party,
if not parliamentary government, with all its vices and mischiefs, will have passed
away, and the absolute Monarchy of the Kingdom of Heaven will have come.

So much, then, is told us of Robert Gordon in few words: 'A single-hearted
and painful Christian, much employed in parliaments and public meetings.' To
which may be added this extract taken out of the Minute Book of the Covenanters'
War Committee: 'The same day there was delyverit to the said commissioners by
Robert Gordoun of Knockbrax sex silver spoones Scots worke, weightan vi. unce
xii. dropes.' Had Knockbrex also, like the Earlstons, been fined by the bishops and
harried by the dragoons till he had nothing left to deliver to the Commissioners
but six silver spoons and a single heart? It would seem so. Like the woman in the
Gospel, Gordon gave to the Covenant all that he had. Had Robert Gordon been a
Highlander instead of a Lowlander; had he been a Ross-shire crofter instead of a
small laird in Wigtown, he would have been one of the foremost of the well-known
'men.' His temperament and his experiences would have made him a prince among
the ministers and the men of the far north. Were it nothing else, the pains he spent
on the growth of the life of grace in his own soul,--that would have canonised him
among the saintliest of those saintly men. He would have set the Question on many
a Communion Friday, and the Question in his hands would not have concerned
itself with surface matters. Was it because Rutherford had now gone nearer that

great region of experimental casuistry that he started that excellent Friday problem in a letter from Aberdeen to Knockbrex in 1637? With Rutherford everything,--the most doctrinal, experimental, ecclesiastical, political, all--ran always up into Christ, His love and His loveableness. 'Is Christ more to be loved for gaining for us justification or sanctification?' Such was one of the questions Rutherford set to his correspondent in the south. Did any of you north-country folk ever hear that question debated out before one of your Highland communions? If you care to see how Rutherford the minister and Knockbrex the man debated out their debt to Jesus Christ, read the priceless correspondence that passed between them, and especially, read the 170th Letter. But first, and before that, do you either know, or care to know, what either justification or sanctification is? When you do know and do care for these supreme things, then you too will in time become a single-hearted and painstaking Christian like Robert Gordon, or else an ecstatic and enraptured Christian like Samuel Rutherford. And that again will be very much according to your natural temperament, your attainments, and your experiences. And nothing in this world will thereafter interest and occupy you half so much as just those questions that are connected first with all that Christ is in Himself and all that He has done for you, and then with the signs and the fruits of the life of grace in your own souls.

# XIV.  JOHN GORDON OF RUSCO

'Remember these seven things.'-- **Rutherford**.

There were plenty of cold Covenanters, as they were called, in Kirkcudbright in John Gordon's day, but the laird of Rusco was not one of them.  Rusco Castle was too near Anwoth Kirk and Anwoth Manse, and its owner had had Samuel Rutherford too long for his minister and his near neighbour to make it possible for him to be 'ane cold covenanter quha did not do his dewtie in everything committed to his charge thankfullie and willinglie.'  We find Gordon of Rusco giving good reasons indeed, as he thought, why he should not be sent out of the Stewartry on the service of the covenant, but the war committee 'expelled his resounes' and instantly commanded his services.  And from all we can gather out of the old Minute Book, Rusco played all the noble part that Rutherford expected of him in the making of Scotland and in the salvation of her kirk.

Like the Psalmist in the hundred and second Psalm, we take pleasure in the stones of Rusco Castle, and we feel a favour to the very dust thereof.  Even in Rutherford's day that rugged old pile was sacred and beautiful to the eyes of Rutherford and his people, because of what the grace of God had wrought within its walls; and, both for that, and for much more like that, both in Rutherford's own day and after it, we also look with awe and with desire at the ruined old mansion-house.  A hundred years before John Gordon bade Rusco farewell for heaven, we find a friend of John Knox's on his deathbed there, and having a departure from his deathbed administered to him there as confident and as full of a desire to depart as John Knox's own.  'The Last and Heavenly Speeches of John, Viscount Kenmure' also still echo through the deserted rooms of Rusco, and after he had gone up from it we find still another Gordon there with his wife and children and farm-tenants, all warm Covenanters, and all continuing the Rusco tradition of godliness and virtue. At the same time Samuel Rutherford was not the man to take it for granted that John Gordon and his household were all saved and home in heaven because they lived within such sacred walls and were all church members and warm Covenanters. He was only the more anxious about the Gordon family because they had such an ancestry and were all bidding so fair to leave behind them such a posterity. And thus it is that, from his isle of Patmos, Samuel Rutherford, like the apostle John to his seven churches, sends to John Gordon seven things that are specially to be remembered and laid to heart by the laird of Rusco.

1. Remember, in the first place, my dear brother, those most solemn and too much forgotten words of our Lord, that there are but few that be saved. Is that really so? said a liberal-minded listener to our Lord one day. Is that really so, that there are but few that be saved? Mind your own business, was our Lord's answer. For there are many lost by making their own and other men's salvation a matter of dialectic and debate in the study and in the workshop rather than of silence, and godly fear, and a holy life. Yes, there are few that be saved, said Samuel Rutherford, writing again the same year to Farmer Henderson, who occupied the home- stead-ing of Rusco. Men go to heaven in ones and twos. And that you may go there, even if it has to be alone, love your enemies and stand to the truth I taught you. Fear no man, fear God only. Seek Christ every day. You will find Him alone in the fields of Rusco. Seek a broken heart for sin, for, otherwise, you may seek Him all your days, but you will never find Him. And it is not in our New Testament only, and in such books as Rutherford's **Letters** only, that we are reminded of the loneliness of our road to heaven; in a hundred places in the wisest and deepest books of the heathen world we read the same warning; notably in the Greek Tablet of Cebes, which reads almost as if it had been cut out of the Sermon on the Mount. 'Do you not see,' says the old man, 'a little door, and beyond the door a way which is not much crowded, for very few are going along it, it is so difficult of access, so rough, and so stony?' 'Yes,' answers the stranger. 'And does there not seem,' subjoins the old man, 'to be a high hill and the road up it very narrow, with precipices on each side? Well, that is the way that leads to the true instruction.' 'A cause is not good,' says Rutherford in another of his pungent books, 'because it is followed by many. Men come to Zion in ones and twos out of a whole tribe, but they go to hell in their thousands. The

way to heaven is overgrown with grass; there are the traces of but few feet on that way, only you may see here and there on it the footprints of Christ's bloody feet to let you know that you are not gone wrong but are still on the right way.'

2. Remember also that other word of our Lord,--that heaven is like a fortress in this, that it must be taken by force. Only our Lord means that the force must not be done to the gates or the walls of heaven, but to our own hard hearts and evil lives. 'I find it hard to be a Christian,' writes Rutherford to Rusco. 'There is no little thrusting and thringing to get in at heaven's gates. Heaven is a strong castle that has to be taken by force.' 'Oh to have one day more in my pulpit in Aberdeen!' cried a great preacher of that day when he was dying. 'What would you do?' asked another minister who sat at his bedside. 'I would preach to the people the difficulty of salvation,' said the dying man. 'Remember,' wrote Rutherford to Rusco from the same city, 'Remember that it is violent sweating and striving that alone taketh heaven.'

3. Remember also that there are many who start well at the bottom of the hill who never get to the top. We ministers and elders know that only too well; we do not need to be reminded of that. There are the names of scores and scores of young communicants on our session books of whom we well remember how we boasted about them when they took the foot of the hill, but we never mention their names now, or only with a blush and in a whisper. Some take to the hill-foot at one age, and some at another; some for one reason and some for another. A bereavement awakens one, a sickness--their own or that of some one dear to them--another; a disappointment in love or in business will sometimes do it; a fall into sin will also do it; a good book, a good sermon, a conversation with a friend who has been some way up the hill; many things may be made use of to make men and women, and young men and women, take a start toward a better life and a better world. But for ten, for twenty, who so start not two ever come to the top. 'Heaven is not next door,' writes Rutherford to Rusco; 'if it were we would all be saved.' There was a well-known kind of Christians in Rutherford's day that the English Puritans called by the nickname of the Temporaries; and it is to pluck Rusco from among them that Rutherford writes to him this admonitory letter. And there is an equally well-known type of Christian in our day, though I do not know that any one has so happily nicknamed him as yet.

'The Scriptures beguiled the Pharisees,' writes Rutherford; and the Christian

I refer to is self-beguiled with the very best things in the Scriptures. The cross is always in his mouth, but you will never find it on his back. He has got, at least in language, as far as the cross, but he remains there. He says the burden is off his back, and he takes care that he shall keep out of that kind of life that would put it on again. He has been once pardoned, and he takes his stand upon that. He strove hard till he was converted, and he sometimes strives hard to get other men brought to the same conversion. But his conversion has been all exhausted in the mere etymology of the act, for he has only turned round in his religious life, he has not made one single step of progress. But let one of the greatest masters of true religion that ever taught the Church of Christ speak to us on the subject of this gin-horse Christian. 'The Scriptures,' says Jonathan Edwards, 'everywhere represent the seeking, the striving, and the labour of a Christian as being chiefly to be gone through *after* his conversion, and his conversion as being but the beginning of the work. And almost all that is said in the New Testament of men's watching, giving earnest heed to themselves, running the race that is set before them, striving and agonising, pressing forward, reaching forth, crying to God night and day; I say, almost all that is said in the New Testament of these things is spoken of and is directed to God's saints. Where these things are applied once to sinners seeking salvation, they are spoken of the saint's prosecution of their high calling ten times. But many have got in these days into a strange anti-scriptural way of having all their striving and wrestling over *before* they are converted, and so having an easy time of it afterwards.'

4. Remember, also, wrote Rutherford, to look up the Scriptures and read and lay to heart the lessons of Esau's life and Judas's, of the life of Balaam, and Saul, and Pharaoh, and Simon Magus, and Caiaphas, and Ahab, and Jehu, and Herod, and the man in Matthew viii. 19, and the apostates in Hebrews vi. For all these were at best but watered brass and reprobate silver. 'One day,' writes Mrs. William Veitch of Dumfries in her autobiography, 'having been at prayer, and coming into the room where one was reading a letter of Mr. Rutherford's directed to one John Gordon of Rusco--giving an account of how far one might go and yet prove a hypocrite and miss heaven--it occasioned great exercise in me.' Dr. Andrew Bonar is no doubt entirely right when he says that this letter, now open before us, must have been the heart-searching letter that caused that God-fearing woman, fresh from her knees, so great exercise. Let us share her great exercise, and in due time we shall share her

great salvation. Not otherwise.

5. 'And remember,' he proceeds, 'what your besetting sin may cost you in the end. I beseech you therefore and obtest you in the Lord, to make conscience of all rash and passionate oaths, of raging and avenging anger, of night-drinking, of bad company, of Sabbath-breaking, of hurting any under you by word or deed, of hurting your very enemies. Except you receive the Kingdom of God as a little child, you cannot enter it. That is a word that should make your great spirit fall.' 'If men allow themselves in malice and envy,' writes Thomas Shepard, a contemporary of Rutherford's, 'or in wanton thoughts, that will condemn them, even though their corruptions do not break out in any scandalous way. Such thoughts are quite sufficient evidence of a rotten heart. If a man allows himself in malice or in envy, though he thinks he does it not, yet he is a hypocrite; if in his heart he allows it he cannot be a saint of God. If there be one evil way, though there have been many reformations, the man is an ungodly man. One way of sin is exception enough against any man's salvation. A small shot will kill a man as well as a large bullet, a small leak let alone will sink a ship, and a small, and especially a secret and spiritual sin, will cost a man his soul.'

6. 'Remember, also, your shortening sand-glass.' On the day when John Gordon was born a sand-glass with his name written upon it was filled, and from that moment it began to run down before God in heaven. For how long it was filled God who filled it alone knew. Whether it was filled to run out in an hour, or to run till Gordon was cut down in mid-time of his days, or till he had attained to his threescore years and ten, or whether it was to run on to the labour and sorrow of four-score years, not even his guardian angel knew, but God only. And then beside that sand-glass a leaf, taken out of the seven-sealed book, was laid open, on the top of which was found written the as yet unbaptized name of this new- born child. And under his name was found written all that John Gordon was appointed and expected to do while his sand-glass was still running. His opening life as child and boy and man in Galloway; his entrance on Rusco; his friendship with Samuel Rutherford; his duties to his family, to his tenants, to his Church, and to the Scottish Covenant; the inward life he was commanded and expected to live alone with God; the seven things he was every day to remember; the evangelical graces of heart and life and character he was to be told and to be enabled to put on; the death he was to

die, and the 'freehold' he was after all these things to enter on in heaven. And it is of that sand-glass that was at that moment running so fast and so low within the veil that Rutherford writes so often and so earnestly to the so-forgetful laird of Rusco. And how solemnising it is, if anything would solemnise our hard hearts, that we all have a sand-glass standing before God with our names written upon it, and that it is running out before God day and night unceasingly. We shall all be too suddenly solemnised when the last grain of our measured- out sand has dropped down, and the blind Fury will come, and without pity and without remorse will slit our thin-spun life with her abhorred shears. And that whether our life-work is finished or no, half-finished or no, or not even begun. The night cometh, and the shears with it, when no man can work. Our family must then be left behind us, however they have been brought up; our farm also, however it has been worked; our estate also, however it has been managed; our pulpit, our pew, our church, our character, and even our salvation, and we must, all alone with God, face and account for the empty sand-glass and the accusing book. Is it any wonder that John Gordon's minister, when he was in the spirit in Patmos, should write him as we here read? What kind of a minister would he have been, and what a sand-glass, and what a book of angry account he would have had soon to face himself, if he had let all his people in Anwoth live on and suddenly die in total forgetfulness of the sand and the shears, the book of duty and the book of judgment. 'Remember,' Rutherford wrote, 'remember and misspend not your short sand- glass, for your forenoon is already spent, your afternoon has come, and your night will be on you when you will not see to work. Let your heart, therefore, be set upon finishing your journey and summing up and laying out the accounts of your life and the grounds of your death alone before God.'

7. And, above all, remember that after you have done all, it is the blood of Christ alone that will set you down safely as a freeholder in Heaven. But His blood, and your everyday remembrance of His blood, and your everyday obligation to it, will surely set you, John Gordon of Rusco on earth, so down a freeholder in heaven.

'Soon shall the cup of glory
  Wash down earth's bitterest woes,

Soon shall the desert briar
  Break into Eden's Rose:
I stand upon His merit,
  I know no other stand,
Not e'en where glory dwelleth
  In Immanuel's land.'

# XV. BAILIE JOHN KENNEDY

'Die well.'-- **Rutherford**.

Bailie John Kennedy, of Ayr, was the remarkable son of a remarkable father. Old Hugh Kennedy's death-bed was for long a glorious tradition among the godly in the West of Scotland. The old saint was visited in his last hours on earth with a joy that was unspeakable and full of glory: the mere report of it made an immense impression both on the Church and the world. And his son John, who stood entranced beside his father's chariot of fire, never forgot the transporting sight. He did not need Rutherford's warning never to forget his father's example and his father's end. For John Kennedy was a 'choice Christian,' as a well- known writer of that day calls him. And he was not alone. There were many choice Christians in that day in Scotland. Were there ever more, for its size, in any land or in any church on the face of the earth? I do not believe there ever were. Next to that favoured land that produced the Psalmists and the Prophets, I know no land that, for its numbers, possessed so many men and women of a profoundly spiritual experience, and of an adoring and heavenly mind, as Scotland possessed in the sixteenth and seventeenth centuries. The Wodrow volumes should be studied throughout by every lover of his church and his country, and especially by every student of divinity and church history.

But we need go no further than Samuel Rutherford's letter-bag; for, when we open it, what rich treasures of the religious life pour out of it! What minds and what hearts those men and women had! And how they gave up their whole mind and heart to the life of godliness in the land, and to the life of God in their own hearts! How thin and poor our religious life appears beside theirs! What minister in Scotland to-day could write such letters? And to whom could he address them after they were written? Was it the persecution? Was it the new reformation doctrines? Was it the masculine and Pauline preaching: preaching, say, like Robert Bruce's and Rutherford's that did it? What was it that raised up in Scotland such a crop of ripe and rich saints? Who are these, and whence came they?

Rutherford was always on the outlook for opportunities to employ his private pen for the conversion of sinners, and for the comfort, the upbuilding, and the holiness of God's people. From his manse at Anwoth, from his prison at Aberdeen, from his class-room at St. Andrews, and from the Jerusalem Chamber at Westminster, his letter-bag went out full of those messages, so warm, so tender, so powerful, to his multitudinous correspondents. Public events, domestic joys and sorrows, personal matters, special providences,--to turn them all to a good result Rutherford was always on the watch.

News had come to Rutherford's ears of an almost fatal accident that Kennedy had had through his boat being swept out to sea; and that was too good a chance to lose of trying to touch his correspondent's heart yet more deeply about death, and the due preparation for it. Read his letter to John Kennedy on his deliverance from shipwreck. See with what apostolic dignity and sweetness he salutes Kennedy. See how he lifts up Kennedy's accident out of the hands of winds and waves, and traces it all up to the immediate hand of God. See how he speaks of Kennedy's reprieve from death; and how the spared man should make use of his lengthened days. Altogether, a noble, powerful, apostolic letter; a letter that must have had a great influence in making Bailie Kennedy the choice Christian that he was and that he became. We have only three letters preserved of Rutherford's to Kennedy. But we have sufficient evidence that they were fast and dear friends. Rutherford writes to Kennedy from Aberdeen, upbraiding him for forgetting him; and what a letter that also is! It stands well out among the foremost of his letters for fulness of all the great qualities of Rutherford's intellect and heart.

But it is with the shipwreck letter that we have to do to-night; and with the expressions in it we have taken for our text: 'Die well, for the last tide will ebb fast.' 'It is appointed to all men once to die,' says the Apostle, in a most solemn passage. Think of that, think often of that, think it out, think it through to the end. God has appointed our death. He has our name down in His seven-sealed Book; and when the Lamb opens the Book, and finds the place, He reads our name, and all that is appointed us till death, and after death. The exact and certain time of our death is all appointed; the place of it also; and all the circumstances. Just when it is to happen; to-night, to-morrow, this year, next year, perhaps not this dying century; we shall perhaps live to write A.D. 1901 on our letters. Near or afar off, it is all appointed. And all the circumstances of it also. I don't know why Rutherford should say to Kennedy that it is a terrible thing to 'die in one's day clothes,' unless he hides a parable under that. But whether in day clothes or night clothes; whether like Dr. Andrew Thomson, our first minister, in Melville Street, and with his hand on the latchkey of his own door; or, like Dr. Candlish, his successor, in his bed, and repeating, now Shakespeare, and now the Psalmist; by the upsetting of a boat, the shape in which death came near to Kennedy, or by the upsetting of a coach, as I escaped myself, not being ready. 'The Lord knew,' writes Rutherford, 'that you had forgotten something that was necessary for your journey, and let you go back for it. You had not all your armour on wherewith to meet with the last enemy.' By day or by night; by land or by sea; alone, or surrounded by weeping friends; in rapture like Hugh Kennedy, or in thick darkness like your Lord; all, all is appointed. Just think of it; the types may be cast, the paper may be woven, the ink may be made that is to announce to the world your death and mine. It is all appointed, and we cannot alter it or postpone it. The only thing we have any hand in is this: whether our death, when it comes, is to be a success or a failure; that is to say, whether we shall die well or ill. Since we die but once, then, and since so much turns upon it, let us take advice how we are to do it well. We cannot come back to make a second attempt; if we do not shoot the gulf successfully, we cannot climb back and try the leap again; we die once, and, after death, the judgment. Now, when we have any difficult thing before us, how do we prepare ourselves for it? Do we not practise it as often as we possibly can? If it is running in a race, or wrestling in a match, or playing a tune, or shooting at a target, do we not assiduously practise it? Yes, every sensible man is careful to have his hand and his foot accustomed to the trial before the appointed day comes. Practice makes perfect: practise dying, then, as Rutherford counsels you, and you will make a perfect thing of your death, and not otherwise. But how are we to practise dying? Fore-fancy it, as Rutherford says. Act it over beforehand; die speculatively, as Goodwin says. Say to yourself, Suppose this were death at my door to-night. Suppose he were to visit me in the night, what would I say to him, and what would he say to me?  Make acquaintance with death, Rutherford writes to Lady Kenmure also.  Learn his ways, his manner of approach, his language, and his look.  Conjure him up, practise upon him, have your part rehearsed and ready to be performed.  Let not a heathen be beforehand with you in dying.  Seneca said that every night after his lamp was out, and the house quiet, he went over all his past day, and looked at it all in the light of death.  What he did after that he does not tell us; but Rutherford will tell you if you consult him what you should do.  Well, that is one way of practising dying.  For Sleep is the brother of Death.  And to meet the one brother right will prepare us to meet the other.  Speculate at night, then-- speculate and say, Suppose this were my last night.  Suppose, O my soul, thou wert to cast anchor to- morrow in Eternity, how shouldst thou close thine eyes to-night?  Speculate also at other men's funerals.  When the clod thuds down on their coffin, think yourself inside of it.  When you see the undertaker's man screwing down the lid, suppose it yours.  Take your own way of doing it; only, practise dying, and let not death spring upon you unawares.  Die daily, for, as Dante says, 'The arrow seen beforehand slacks its flight.'

Writing to another old man, Rutherford points out to him the gracious purpose of God in appointing him his death in old age.  'It is,' says Rutherford, 'that you may have full leisure to look over all your accounts and papers before you take ship.'  What a tangle our papers also are in as life goes on; and what need we have of a time of leisure to set things right before we hand them over.  Rutherford, therefore, makes us see old Carlton on his bed with his pillows propping him up, and a drawer open on the bed, and bundles of old letters and bills spread out before him.  Old love letters; old business letters; his mother's letters to him when he was a boy at Edinburgh College; letters in cipher that no human eye can read but those old, bleared, weeping eyes that fill that too late drawer with their tears.  The old voyager is looking over his papers before he takes ship.  And he comes on things he had totally forgotten: debts he had thought paid; petitions he had thought answered; promises he had thought fulfilled; till he calls young Carlton, his son, to his bedside, and tells him things that break both men's hearts to say and to hear; and commits to his son and heir sad duties that should never have been due; debts, promises, obligations, reparations, such that, to remember them, is a terrible experience on an old man's deathbed.  But what mercy that he was not carried off, and his drawer unopened!

Now, speaking of taking ship, when we are preparing for a voyage, and a visit to another country and another city, we 'read up,' as we say, before we set sail. Before we start for Rome we read our Tacitus and our Horace, our Gibbon and our Merivale. If it is Florence we take down Vasari and Dante, Lord Lindsay and Mrs. Jamieson, and so on. Now, if Eternity holds for us a new world, with cities and peoples that are all new to us, should we not prepare ourselves for them also? Have you, then, laid in a library for your old age, when, like old Carlton, you will be lying waiting at the water-side? What books do you read when you wish to put on the mind of a man who intends to die well? 'Read to me where I first cast my anchor,' said John Knox, when dying, to his weeping wife. Does your wife know where you first cast your anchor? Does she know already what to read to you when you are preparing for the last voyage?

And then, having prepared for, and practised dying well, play the man and perform it well when the day comes. 'Die as your father died,' says Rutherford to Kennedy. Now, that is too much to ask of any man, because old Hugh Kennedy's deathbed was what it was by the special grace of God. You cannot command any man to die in rapture. But Rutherford does not mean that, as he is careful to explain. He means, as he says, 'die believing.' It will be your last act as a believer, therefore do it well. You have been practising faith all your days; show that practice makes perfection at the end. As Rutherford said to George Gillespie when he was on his deathbed, 'Hand over all your bills, paid and unpaid, to your surety. Give him the keys of the drawer, and let him clear it out for himself after you are gone.' And then, with the ruling passion strong in death, he added, 'Die not on sanctification but on justification, die not on inherent but on imputed righteousness.' And then, to come to the very last act of all, there is what we call the death-grip. A dying man feels the whole world giving way under him. All he built upon, leaned upon, looked to, is like sliding sand, like sinking water; and he grasps at anything, anybody, the bedpost, the bed-curtains, the bed-clothes, his wife's hand, his son's arm, the very air sometimes. On what, on whom will you seize hold in your last gasp and death-grip?

'Rock of Ages, cleft for me,
Let me hide myself in Thee!'

## XVI.  JAMES GUTHRIE

'The short man who could not bow.'-- ***Cromwell***.

James Guthrie was the son of the laird of that ilk in the county of Angus.  St. Andrews was his ***alma mater***, and under her excellent nurture young Guthrie soon became a student of no common name.  His father had destined him for the Episcopal Church, and, what with his descent from an ancient and influential family, his remarkable talents, and his excellent scholarship, it is not to be wondered at that a bishop's mitre sometimes dangled before his ambitious eyes.  'He was then prelatic,' says Wodrow in his ***Analecta***, 'and strong for the ceremonies.'  But as time went on, young Guthrie's whole views of duty and of promotion became totally changed, till, instead of a bishop's throne, he ended his days on the hangman's ladder.  After having served his college some time as regent or assistant professor in the Moral Philosophy Chair, Guthrie took licence, and was immediately thereafter settled as parish minister of Lauder, in the momentous year 1638.  And when every parish in Scotland sent up its representatives to Edinburgh to subscribe the covenant in Greyfriars Churchyard, the parish of Lauder had the pride of seeing its young minister take his life in his hand, like all the best ministers and truest patriots in the land.  But just as Guthrie was turning in at the gate of the Greyfriars, who should cross the street before him, so as almost to run against him, but the city executioner!  The omen--for it was a day of omens--made the young minister stagger for a moment, but only for a moment.  At the same time the ominous incident made such an impression on the young Covenanter's heart and imagination, that he said to some of his fellow-subscribers as he laid down the pen, 'I know that I shall die for what I have done this day, but I cannot die in a better cause.'

In the lack of better authorities we are compelled to trace the footsteps of James

Guthrie through the Laodicean pages of Robert Baillie for several years to come. Baillie did not like Guthrie, and there was no love lost between the two men. The one man was all fire together in every true and noble cause, and the other we spew out of our mouth at every page of his indispensable book. As Carlyle says, Baillie contrived to 'carry his dish level' through all that terrible jostle of a time. And accordingly while we owe Baillie our very grateful thanks that he kept such a diary, and carried on such an extensive and regular correspondence during all that distracted time, we owe him no other thanks. He carried his dish level, and he had his reward.

As we trace James Guthrie's passionate footsteps for the years to come through Principal Baillie's sufficiently gossiping, but not unshrewd, pages, we soon see that he is travelling fast and sure toward the Nether Bow. We hear continually from our time-serving correspondent of Guthrie's 'public invective,' of his 'passionate debates,' of his 'venting of his mind,' of his 'peremptory letters,' of his 'sharp writing,' and of his being 'rigid as ever,' and so on. All that about his too zealous co-presbyter, and then his fulsome eulogy of the returning king--his royal wisdom, his moderation, his piety, and his grave carriage--as also what he says of 'the conspicuous justice of God in hanging up the bones of Oliver Cromwell, the disgracing of the two Goodwins, blind Milton, John Owen, and others of that maleficent crew,' all crowned with the naive remark that 'the wisest and best are quiet till they see whither these things will go'--it is plain that while our wise and good author is carrying his dish as level as the uneven roads will allow, Guthrie is as plainly carrying his head straight to the Cross of Edinburgh, and to the iron spikes of the Canongate.

All the untold woes of that so woful time came of the sword of the civil power being still grafted on the crook of the Church; as also of the insane attempt of so many of our forefathers to solder the crown of Charles Stuart to the crown of Jesus Christ. How those two so fatal, and not even yet wholly remedied, mistakes, brought Argyll to the block and Guthrie to the ladder in one day in Edinburgh, we read in the instructive and inspiriting histories of that terrible time; and we have no better book on that time for the mass of readers than just honest John Howie's **Scots Worthies**. There is a passage in our Scottish martyr's last defence of himself that has always reminded me of Socrates' similar defence before the judges of Athens.

'My lords,' said Guthrie, 'my conscience I cannot submit. But this old and crazy body I do submit, to do with it whatsoever you will; only, I beseech you to ponder well what profit there is likely to be in my blood. It is not the extinguishing of me, or of many more like me, that will extinguish the work of reformation in Scotland. My blood will contribute more for the propagation of the Covenant and the full reformation of the kirk than my life and liberty could do, though I should live on for many years.' One can hardly help thinking that Guthrie must have been reading *The Apology* in his manse in Stirling at the moment he was apprehended. But in the case of Guthrie, as in the case of Socrates, no truth, no integrity, and no eloquence could save him; for, as Bishop Burnet frankly says, 'It was resolved to make a public example of a Scottish minister, and so Guthrie was singled out. I saw him suffer,' the Bishop adds, 'and he was so far from showing any fear that he rather expressed a contempt of death.' James Cowie, his precentor, and beadle, and body-servant, also saw his master suffer, and, like Bishop Burnet, he used to tell the impression that his old master's last days made upon him. 'When he had received sentence of death,' Cowie told Wodrow's informant, 'he came forth with a kind of majesty, and his face seemed truly to shine.' It needed something more than this world could supply to make a man's face to shine under the sentence that he be hanged at the Cross of Edinburgh, his body dismembered, and his head fixed on an iron spike in the West Port of the same city. The disgraceful and ghastly story of his execution, and the hacking up of his body, may all be read in Howie, beside a picture of the Nether Bow as it still stands in our Free Church and Free State Day. 'Art not Thou from everlasting, O Lord my God?' were James Guthrie's last words as he stood on the ladder. 'O mine Holy One: I shall not die, but live. Now lettest Thou Thy servant depart in peace; for mine eyes have seen Thy salvation.'

There is one fine outstanding feature that has always characterised and distinguished the whole of the Rutherford circle in our eyes, and that is their deep, keen Pauline sense of sin. Without this, all their patriotism, all their true statesmanship, and even all their martyrdom for the sake of the truth, would have had, comparatively speaking, little or no interest for us. What think ye of sin? is the crucial question we put to any character, scriptural or ecclesiastical, who claims our time and our attention. If they are right about sin, they are all the more likely to be right about everything else; and if they are either wrong or only shallow about sin, their teaching and their experience on other matters are not likely to be of much value or much interest to us. We have had written over our portals against all comers: Know thyself if thou wouldst either interest us or benefit us, or with the understanding and the spirit worship with us. And all the true Rutherford circle, without one exception, have known the true secret and have given the true password. Their keen sense and scriptural estimate of the supreme evil of sin first made them correspondents of Rutherford's; and as that sense and estimate grew in them they passed on into an inner and a still more inner circle of those Scottish saints and martyrs who corresponded with Rutherford, and closed, with so much honour and love, around him. And the two Guthries, James and William, as we shall see, were famous even in that day for their praying and for their preaching about sin.

There is an excellent story told of James Guthrie's family worship in the manse of Stirling, that bears not unremotely on the matter we have now on hand. Guthrie was wont to pray too much, both at the family altar and in the pulpit, as if he had been alone with his own heart and God. And he carried that bad habit at last to such a length in his family, that he almost drove poor James Cowie, his manservant, out of his senses, till when Cowie could endure no longer to be singled out and exposed and denounced before the whole family, he at last stood up with some boldness before his master and demanded to be told out, as man to man, and not in that cruel and injurious way, what it was he had done that made his master actually every day thus denounce and expose him. 'O James, man, pardon me, pardon me. I was, I see now, too much taken up with my own heart and its pollutions to think enough of you and the rest.' 'It was that, and the like of that,' witnessed Cowie, 'that did me and my wife more good than all my master's well-studied sermons.' The intimacy and tenderness of the minister and his man went on deeper and grew closer, till at the end we find Cowie reading to him at his own request the Epistle to the Romans, and when the reader came to the passage, 'I will have mercy on whom I will have mercy,' the listener burst into tears, and exclaimed, 'James, James, halt there, for I have nothing but that to lippen to.' And then, on the ladder, and before a great crowd of Edinburgh citizens: 'I own that I am a sinner--yea, and one of the vilest that ever made a profession of religion. My corruptions have been strong and many, and they have made me a sinner in all things--yea, even in following my duty. But blessed be God, who hath showed His mercy to such a wretch, and hath revealed His Son unto me, and made me a minister of the everlasting Gospel, and hath sealed my ministry on the hearts of not a few of His people.' James Guthrie's ruling passion, as Cowie remarked, was still strong in his death.

On one occasion Guthrie and some of his fellow-ministers were comparing experiences and confessing to one another their 'predominant sins,' and when it came to Guthrie's turn he told them that he was much too eager to die a violent death. For, said he, I would like to die with all my wits about me. I would not like eyesight and memory and reason and faith all to die out on my deathbed and leave me to tumble into eternity bereft of them all. Guthrie was greatly afraid at the thought of death, but it was the premature death of his reason, and even of his faith, that so much alarmed and horrified him to think of. He envied the men who kneeled down on the scaffold, or leaped off the ladder, in full possession at the last moment of all their senses and all their graces. 'Give me a direct answer, sir,' demanded Dr. Johnson of his physician when on his deathbed. . . . 'Then I will take no more opiates, for I have prayed that I may be able to render up my soul to God unclouded.' And when pressed by his attendants to take some generous nourishment, he replied almost with his last breath, 'I will take anything but inebriating sustenance.'

But in nothing was good James Guthrie's tenderness to sin better seen than in the endless debates and dissensions of which that day was so full. So sensitive was he to the pride and the anger and the ill-will that all controversy kindles in our hearts that, as soon as he felt any unholy heat in his own heart, or saw it in the hearts of the men he debated with, he at once cut short the controversy with some such words as these: 'We have said too much on this matter already; let us leave it till we love one another more.' If hot-blooded Samuel Rutherford had sat more at James Guthrie's feet in the matter of managing a controversy, his name would have been almost too high and too spotless for this present life. Samuel Rutherford's one vice, temper, was one of James Guthrie's chief virtues.

We have only two, or at most three, of the many letters that must have passed between Rutherford and Guthrie preserved to us. And, as is usual with Rutherford when he writes to any member of his innermost circle, he writes to Guthrie so as still more completely to win his heart. And in nothing does dear Rutherford win all our hearts more than in his deep humility, and quick, keen sense of his own inability and utter unworthiness. 'I am at a low ebb,' he writes to Guthrie from the

Jerusalem Chamber, 'yea, as low as any gracious soul can possibly be. Shall I ever see even the borders of the good land above?' I read that fine letter again last Sabbath afternoon in my room at hospitable Helenslee, overlooking the lower reaches of the Clyde, and as I read this passage, I recollected the opportune sea-view commanded by my window. I had only to rise and look out to see an excellent illustration of my much- exercised author; for the forenoon tide had just retreated to the sea, and the broad bed of the river was left by the retreated tide less a river than a shallow, clammy channel. Shoals of black mud ran out from our shore, meeting and mingling with shoals of black mud from the opposite shore. There was scarce clean water enough to float the multitude of buoys that dipped and dragged in their bed of mire. That any ship, to call a ship, could ever work its way up that sweltering sewer seemed an utter impossibility. There was Rutherford's low ebb, then, under my very eyes. There was low water indeed. And the low water seemed to laugh the waiting seamen's hopes to scorn. But next morning my heart rose high as I looked out at my window and saw all the richly-laden vessels lighting their fires and spreading their sails, and setting their faces to the replenished river. And I thought of Samuel Rutherford's ship, far past all her ebbing tides now, and for ever anchored in her haven above.

On the wall of my room in the same beautiful house there was a powerful cartoon of Peter's crucifixion, head downwards, for his Master's sake. The masterpiece of Filippino Lippi I felt to be an excellent illustration also of Rutherford's letter to James Guthrie and the rest of the ministers and elders who were imprisoned in the Castle of Edinburgh for daring to remind Charles Stuart of the contents of the Covenant to which both he and the whole nation had solemnly sworn. 'If Christ doth own me,' Rutherford wrote to the martyrs in the Castle, 'let me be laid in my grave in a bloody winding-sheet; let me go from the scaffold to the spikes in four quarters--grave or no grave, as He pleases, if only He but owns me.' And I seemed to see the crucified disciple's glorified Master appearing over his reversed cross and saying, 'Thou art Peter, and with this thy blood I will sow widespread my Church.' Yes, my brethren, if Christ but owns us, that will far more than make up to us in a moment for all our imprisonments, and all our martyrdoms, and all our ebbing tides down here. 'Angels, men, and Zion's elders eye us in all our suffering for Christ's sake, but what of all these? Christ is by us, and looketh on, and writeth it all up Himself.'

James Guthrie was hanged and dismembered at the Cross of Edinburgh on the first day of June, 1661. His snow-white head was cut off, and was fixed on a spike in the Nether Bow. James Guthrie got that day that which he had so often prayed for--a sudden plunge into everlasting life with all his senses about him and all his graces at their brightest and their keenest exercise.

---

# XVII. WILLIAM GUTHRIE

'A merry heart doeth good like a medicine.'-- **Solomon**.

William Guthrie was a great humorist, a great sportsman, a great preacher, and a great writer. The true Guthrie blood has always had a drop of humour in it, and the first minister of Fenwick was a genuine Guthrie in this respect. The finest humour springs up out of a wide and a deep heart, and it always has its roots watered at a wellhead of tears. 'William Guthrie was a great melancholian,' says Wodrow, and as we read that we are reminded of some other great melancholians, such as Blaise Pascal and John Foster and William Cowper. William Guthrie knew, by his temperament, and by his knowledge of himself and of other men, that he was a great melancholian, and he studied how to divert himself sometimes in order that he might not be altogether drowned with his melancholy. And thus, maugre his melancholy, and indeed by reason of it, William Guthrie was a great humorist. He was the life of the party on the moors, in the manse, and in the General Assembly. But the life of the party when he was present was always pure and noble and pious, even if it was sometimes somewhat hilarious and boisterous. 'If a man's melancholy temperament is sanctified,' says Rutherford in his **Covenant of Grace**, 'it becomes to him a seat of sound mortification and of humble walking.' And that was the happy result of all William Guthrie's melancholy; it was always alleviated and relieved by great outbursts of good-humour; but both his melancholy and his hilarity always ended in a humbler walk. Samuel Rutherford confides in a letter to his old friend, Alexander Gordon, that he knows a man who sometimes wonders to see any one laugh or sport in this so sinful and sad life. But that was because he had embittered the springs of laughter in himself by the wormwood sins of his youth. William Guthrie had no such remorseful memories continually taking him by the throat as his divinity professor had, and thus it was that with all his melancholy he was known as the greatest humorist and the greatest sportsman in the Scottish Kirk of his day. No doubt he sometimes felt and confessed that his love of fun and frolic was a temptation that he had to watch well against. In his *Saving Interest* he speaks of some sins that are wrought up into a man's natural humour and constitution, and are thus as a right hand and a right eye to him. 'My merriment!' he confessed to one who had rebuked him for it, 'I know all you would say, and my merriment costs me many a salt tear in secret.' At the same time this was often remarked with wonder in Guthrie, that however boisterous his fun was, in one moment he could turn from it to the most serious things. 'It was often observed,' says Wodrow, 'that, let Mr. Guthrie be never so merry, he was presently in a frame for the most spiritual duty, and the only account I can give of it,' says wise Wodrow, 'is, that he acted from spiritual principles in all he did, and even in his relaxations.' Poor Guthrie had a terrible malady that preyed on his most vital part continually--a malady that at last carried him off in the mid- time of his days, and, like Solomon in the proverb, he took to a merry heart as an alleviating medicine. Like our own Thomas Guthrie, too, William Guthrie was a great angler. He could gaff out a salmon in as few minutes as the deftest-handed gamekeeper in all the country, and he could stalk down a deer in as few hours as my lord himself who did nothing else. When he was composing his *Saving Interest*, he somehow heard of a poor countryman near Haddington who had come through some extraordinary experiences in his spiritual life, and he set out from Fenwick all the way to Haddington to see and converse with the much-experienced man. All that night and all the next day Guthrie could not tear himself away from the conversation of the man and his wife. But at last, looking up and down the country, his angling eye caught sight of a trout-stream, and, as if he had in a moment forgotten all about his book at home and all that this saintly man had contributed to it, Guthrie asked him if he had a fishing-rod, and if he would give him a loan of it. The old man felt that his poor rough tackle was to be absolutely glorified by such a minister as Guthrie condescending to touch it, but his good wife did not like this come-down at the end of such a visit as his has been, and she said so. She was a clever old woman, and I am not sure but she had the best of it in the debate that followed about ministers fishing, and about their facetious conversation. The Haddington stream, and the dispute that rose out of it, recall to my mind a not unlike incident that took place in the street of Ephesus, in the far East, just about 1800 years ago. John, the venerable Apostle, had just finished the four-teenth chapter of his great Gospel, and felt himself unable to recollect and write out any more that night. And coming out into the setting sun he began to amuse him-self with a tame partridge that the Bactrian convert had caught and made a present of to his old master. The partridge had been waiting till the pen and the parchment were put by, and now it was on John's hand, and now on his shoulder, and now circling round his sportful head, till you would have thought that its owner was the idlest and foolishest old man in all Ephesus. A huntsman, who greatly respected his old pastor, was passing home from the hills and was sore distressed to see such a saint as John was trifling away his short time with a stupid bird. And he could not keep from stopping his horse and saying so to the old Evangelist. 'What is that you carry in your hand?' asked John at the huntsman with great meekness. 'It is my bow with which I shoot wild game up in the mountains,' replied the huntsman. 'And why do you let it hang so loose? You cannot surely shoot anything with your bow in that condition!' 'No,' answered the amused huntsman, 'but if I always kept my bow strung it would not rebound and send home my arrow when I needed it. I unstring my bow on the street that I may the better shoot with it when I am up among my quarry.' 'Good,' said the Evangelist, 'and I have learned a lesson from you huntsmen. For I am playing with my partridge to-night that I may the better finish my Gospel to-morrow. I am putting everything out of my mind to-night that I may to-morrow the better recollect and set down a prayer I heard offered up by my Master, now more than fifty years ago.' We readers of the Fourth Gospel do not know how much we owe to the Bactrian boy's tame partridge, and neither John Owen nor Thomas Chalmers knew how much they owed to the fishing-rods and curling-stones, the fowling-pieces and the violins that crowded the corners of the manse of Fenwick. I do not know that William Guthrie made a clean breast to the Presbytery of all the reasons that moved him to refuse so many calls to a city charge, though I think I see that David Dickson, the Moderator, divined some of them by the joke he made about the moors of Fenwick to one of the defeated and departing deputations. William Guthrie, the eldest son and sole heir of the laird of Pitforthy, might have had fishing and shooting to his heart's content on his own lands of Pitforthy and Easter Ogle had he not determined, when under Rutherford at St. Andrews, to give himself up wholly to his preaching. But, to put himself out of the temptation that hills and streams and lochs and houses and lands would have been to a man of his tastes and temperament, soon after his conversion William made over to a younger brother all his possessions and all his responsibilities connected therewith, in order that he might give himself up wholly to his preaching. And his reward was that he soon became, by universal consent, the greatest practical preacher in broad Scotland. He could not touch Rutherford, his old professor, at pure theology; he had neither Rutherford's learning, nor his ecstatic eloquence, nor his surpassing love of Jesus Christ, but for handling broken bones and guiding an anxious inquirer no one could hold the candle to William Guthrie. Descriptions of his preaching abound in the old books, such as this: A Glasgow merchant was compelled to spend a Sabbath in Arran, and though he did not understand Gaelic, he felt he must go to the place of public worship. Great was his delight when he saw William Guthrie come into the pulpit. And he tells us that though he had heard in his day many famous preachers, he had never seen under any preacher so much concern of soul as he saw that day in Arran, under the minister of Fenwick. There was scarcely a dry eye in the whole church. A gentleman who was well known as a most dissolute liver was in the church that day, and could not command himself, so deeply was he moved under Guthrie's sermon. That day was remembered long afterwards when that prodigal son had become an eminent Christian man. We see at one time a servant girl coming home from Guthrie's church saying that she cannot contain all that she has heard to-day, and that she feels as if she would need to hear no more on this side heaven. Another day Wodrow's old mother has been at Fenwick, and comes home saying that the first prayer was more than enough for all her trouble without any sermon at all. 'He had a taking and a soaring gift of preaching,' but it was its intensely practical character that made Guthrie's pulpit so powerful and so popular. The very fact that he could go all the way in those days from Fenwick to Haddington, just to have a case of real soul-exercise described to him by the exercised man himself, speaks volumes as to the secret of Guthrie's power in the pulpit. His people felt that their minister knew them; he knew himself, and therefore he knew them. He did not pronounce windy orations about things that did not concern or edify them. He was not learned in the pulpit, nor eloquent, or, if he was--and he was both--all his talents, and all his scholarship, and all his eloquence were forgotten in the intensely practical turn that his preaching immediately took. All the broken hearts in the west country, all those whose sins had found them out, all those who had learned to know the plague of their own heart, and who were passing under a searching sanctification--all such found their way from time to time from great distances to the Kirk of Fenwick. From Glasgow they came, and from Paisley, and from Hamilton, and from Lanark, and from Kilbride, and from many other still more distant places. The lobbies of Fenwick Kirk were like the porches of Bethesda with all the blind, halt, and withered from the whole country round about. After Hutcheson of the *Minor Prophets* had assisted at the communion of Fenwick on one occasion, he said that, if there was a church full of God's saints on the face of the earth, it was at Fenwick communion-table. Pitforthy and Glen Ogle, and all the estates in Angus, were but dust in the balance compared with one Sabbath-day's exercise of such a preaching gift as that of William Guthrie. 'There is no man that hath forsaken houses and lands for My sake and the Gospel's, but shall receive an hundredfold now in this life, and in the world to come life everlasting.'

But further, besides being a great humorist and a great sportsman and a great preacher, William Guthrie was a great writer. A great writer is not a man who fills our dusty shelves with his forgotten volumes. It is not given to any man to fill a whole library with first-rate work. Our greatest authors have all written little books. Job is a small book, so is the Psalms, so is Isaiah, so is the Gospel of John, so is the Epistle to the Romans, so is the *Confessions*, so is the *Comedy*, so is the *Imitation*, so are the *Pilgrim* and the *Grace Abounding*, and though William Guthrie's small book is not for a moment to be ranked with such master-pieces as these, yet it is a small book on a great subject, and a book to which I cannot find a second among the big religious books of our day. You will all find out your own favourite books according to your own talents and tastes. My calling a book great is nothing to you. But it may at least interest you for the passing moment to be told what two men like John Owen, in the seventeenth century, and Thomas Chalmers, in the nineteenth, said about William Guthrie's one little book. Said John Owen, drawing a little gilt copy of *The Great Interest* out of his pocket, 'That author I take to be one of the greatest divines that ever wrote. His book is my *vade mecum*. I carry it always with me. I have written several folios, but there is more divinity in this little book than in them all.' Believe John Owen. Believe all that he says about Guthrie's *Saving Interest*; but do not believe what he says about his own maligned folios till you have read twenty times over his *Person and Glory of Christ*, his *Holy Spirit*, his *Spiritual-mindedness*, and his *Mortification, Dominion, and Indwelling of Sin*. Then hear Dr. Chalmers: 'I am on the eve of finishing Guthrie, which I think is the best book I ever read.' After you have read it, if you ever do, the likelihood is that you will feel as if somehow you had not read the right book when you remember what Owen and Chalmers have said about it. Yes, you have read the right enough book; but the right book has not yet got in you the right reader. There are not many readers abroad like Dr. John Owen and Dr. Thomas Chalmers.

In its style William Guthrie's one little book is clear, spare, crisp, and curt. Indeed, in some places it is almost too spare and too curt in its bald simplicity. True students will not be deterred from it when I say that it is scientifically and experimentally exact in its treatment of the things of the soul. They will best understand and appreciate this statement of Guthrie's biographer that 'when he was working at his *Saving Interest* he endeavoured to inform himself of all the Christians in the country who had been under great depths of exercise, or were still under such depths, and endeavoured to converse with them.' Guthrie is almost as dry as Euclid himself, and almost as severe, but, then, he demonstrates almost with mathematical demonstration the all-important things he sets out to prove. There is no room for rhetoric on a finger- post; in a word, and, sometimes without a word, a finger-post tells you the right way to take to get to your journey's end. And many who have wandered into a far country have found their way home again under William Guthrie's exact marks, clear evidences, and curt directions. You open the little book, and there is a sentence of the plainest, directest, and least entertaining or attractive prose, followed up with a text of Scripture to prove the plain and indisputable prose. Then there is another sentence of the same prose, supported by two texts, and thus the little treatise goes on till, if you are happy enough to be interested in the author's subject-matter, the eternal interests of your own soul, a strong, strange fascination begins to come off the little book and into your understanding, imagination, and heart, till you look up again what Dr. Owen and Dr. Chalmers said about your favourite author, and feel fortified in your valuation of, and in your affection for, William Guthrie and his golden little book.

# XVIII.  GEORGE GILLESPIE

'Our apprehensions are not canonical.'-- *Rutherford*.

George Gillespie was one of that remarkable band of statesmanlike ministers that God gave to Scotland in the seventeenth century.  Gillespie died while yet a young man, but before he died, as Rutherford wrote to him on his deathbed, he had done more work for his Master than many a hundred grey-headed and godly ministers.  Gillespie and Rutherford got acquainted with one another when Rutherford was beginning his work at Anwoth.  In the good providence of God, Gillespie was led to Kenmure Castle to be tutor in the family of Lord and Lady Kenmure, and that threw Rutherford and Gillespie continually together.  Gillespie was still a probationer.  He was ready for ordination, and many congregations were eager to have him, but the patriotic and pure-minded youth could not submit to receive ordination at the hands of the bishops of that day, and this kept him out of a church of his own long after he was ready to begin his ministry.  But the time was not lost to Gillespie himself, or to the Church of Christ in Scotland,--the time that threw Rutherford and Gillespie into the same near neighbourhood, and into intimate and affectionate friendship.  The mere scholarship of the two men would at once draw them together.  They read the same deep books; they reasoned out the same constitutional, ecclesiastical, doctrinal, and experimental problems; till one day, rising off their knees in the woods of Kenmure Castle, the two men took one another by the hand and swore a covenant that all their days, and amid all the trials they saw were coming to Scotland and her Church, they would remain fast friends, would often think of one another, would often name one another before God in prayer, and would regularly write to one another, and that not on church questions only and on the books they were reading, but more especially on the life of God in their own souls. Of the correspondence of those two remarkable men we have only three letters preserved to us, but they are enough to let us see the kind of letters that must have frequently passed between Kenmure Castle and Aberdeen, and between St. Andrews and Edinburgh during the next ten years.

Gillespie was born in the parish manse of Kirkcaldy in 1613; he was ordained to the charge of the neighbouring congregation of Wemyss in 1638, was translated thence to Edinburgh in 1642, and then became one of the four famous deputies who were sent up from the Church of Scotland to sit and represent her in the Westminster Assembly in 1643. Gillespie's great ability was well known, his wide learning and his remarkable controversial powers had been already well proved, else such a young man would never have been sent on such a mission; but his appearance in the debates at Westminster astonished those who knew him best, and won for him a name second to none of the oldest and ablest statesmen and scholars who sat in that famous house. 'That noble youth,' Baillie is continually exclaiming, after each new display of Gillespie's learning and power of argument; 'That singular ornament of our Church'; 'He is one of the best wits of this isle,' and so on. And good John Livingstone, in his wise and sober *Characteristics*, says that, being sent as a Commissioner from the Church of Scotland to the Assembly of Divines at Westminster, Gillespie, 'promoted much the work of reformation, and attained to a gift of clear, strong, pressing, and calm debating above any man of his time.'

Many stories were told in Scotland of the debating powers of young Gillespie as seen on the floor of the Westminster Assembly. Selden was one of the greatest lawyers in England, and he had made a speech one day that both friend and foe felt was unanswerable. One after another of the Constitutional and Evangelical party tried to reply to Selden's speech, but failed. 'Rise, George, man,' said Rutherford to Gillespie, who was sitting with his pencil and note-book beside him. 'Rise, George, man, and defend the Church which Christ hath purchased with His own blood.' George rose, and when he had sat down, Selden is reported to have said to some one who was sitting beside him, 'That young man has swept away the learning and labour of ten years of my life.' Gillespie's Scottish brethren seized upon his note-book to preserve and send home at least the heads of his magnificent speech, but all they found in his little book were these three words: *Da lucem*, *Domine*;

Give light, O Lord. Rutherford had foreseen all this from the days when Gillespie and he talked over Aquinas and Calvin and Hooker and Amesius and Zanchius as they took their evening walks together on the sands of the Solway Firth. It is told also that when the Committee of Assembly was engaged on the composition of the Shorter Catechism, and had come to the question, What is God? like the able men they were, they all shrank from attempting an answer to such an unfathomable question. In their perplexity they asked Gillespie to offer prayer for help, when he began his prayer with these words: 'O God, Thou art a Spirit, infinite, eternal, and unchangeable in Thy being, wisdom, power, holiness, justice, goodness, and truth.' As soon as he said Amen, his opening sentences were remembered, and taken down, and they stand to this day the most scriptural and the most complete answer to that unanswerable question that we have in any creed or catechism of the Christian Church.

As her best tribute to the talents and services of her youngest Commissioner, the Edinburgh Assembly of 1648 appointed Gillespie her Moderator; but his health was fast failing, and he died in the December of that year, in the thirty-sixth year of his age. The inscription on his tombstone at Kirkcaldy ends with these sober and true words: 'A man profound in genius, mild in disposition, acute in argument, flowing in eloquence, unconquered in mind. He drew to himself the love of the good, the envy of the bad, and the admiration of all.' Such was the life and work of George Gillespie, one of the most intimate and confidential correspondents of Samuel Rutherford;--for it was to him that Rutherford wrote the words now before us, 'Our apprehensions are not canonical.'

Every line of life has its own language, its own peculiar vocabulary, that none but its experts, and those who have been brought up to it, know. Go up to the Parliament House and you will hear the advocates and judges talking to one another in a professional speech that the learned layman no more than the ignorant can understand. Our doctors, again, have a shorthand symbolism that only themselves and the chemists understand. And so it is with every business and profession; each several trade strikes out a language for itself. And so does divinity, and, especially, experimental divinity, of which Rutherford's letters are full. We not only need a glossary for the obsolete Scotch, but we need the most simple and everyday expressions of the things of the soul explained to us till once we begin to speak and to write those expressions ourselves. There are judges and advocates and doctors and specialists of all kinds among us who will only be able to make a far-off guess at the meaning of my text, just as I could only make a far-off guess at some of their trade texts. This technical term, 'apprehension,' does not once occur in the Bible, and only once or twice in Shakespeare. 'Our death is most in apprehension,' says that master of expression; and, again, he says that 'we cannot outfly our apprehensions.' And Milton has it once in *Samson*, who says:--

'Thoughts, my tormentors, armed with deadly stings,
Mangle my apprehensive tenderest parts.'

But, indeed, we all have the thing in us, though we may never have put its proper name upon it. We all know what a forecast of evil is--a secret fear that evil is coming upon us. It lays hold of our heart, or of our conscience, as the case may be, and will not let go its hold. And then the heart and the conscience run out continually and lay hold of the future evil and carry it home to our terrified bosoms. We apprehend the coming evil, and feel it long before it comes. We die, like the coward, many times before our death.

Now, Rutherford just takes that well-known word and applies it to his fears and his sinkings of heart about his past sins, and about the unsettled wages of his sins. His conscience makes him a coward, till he thinks every bush an officer. But then he reasons and remonstrates with himself in his deep and intimate letter to Gillespie, and says that these his doubts, and terrors, and apprehensions are not canonical. He is writing to a divine and a scholar, as well as to an experienced Christian man, and he uses words that such scholars and such Christian men quite well understand and like to make use of. The canon that he here refers to is the Holy Scriptures; they are the rule of our faith, and they are also the rule of God's faithfulness. What God has said to us in His word, that we must believe and hold by; that, and not our deserts or our apprehensions, must rule and govern our faith and our trust, just as God's word will be the rule and standard of His dealings with us. His word rules us in our faith and life; and again it rules Him also in His dealings with our faith and with our life. God does not deal with us as we deserve; He does not deal with us as we, in our guilty apprehensions, fear He will. He deals with the apprehensive, penitent, believing sinner according to the grace and the truth of His word. His promises are canonical to Him, not our apprehensions.

Thomas Goodwin, that perfect prince of pulpit exegetes, lays down this canon, and continually himself acts upon it, that 'the context of a scripture is half its interpretation; . . . if a man would open a place of scripture, he should do it rationally; he should go and consider the words before and the words after.' Now, let us apply this rule to the interpretation of this text out of Rutherford, and look at the context, before and after, out of which it is taken.

Remembering his covenant with young Gillespie in the woods of Kenmure, Rutherford wrote of himself to his friend, and said:--'At my first entry on my banishment here my apprehensions worked despairingly upon my cross.' By that he means, and Gillespie would quite well understand his meaning, that his banishment from his work threw him in upon his conscience, and that his conscience whispered to him that he had been banished from his work because of his sins. God is angry with you, his conscience said; He does not love you, He has not forgiven you. But his sanctified good sense, his deep knowledge of God's word, and of God's ways with His people, came to his rescue, and he went on to say to Gillespie that our apprehensions are not canonical. No, he says, our apprehensions tell lies of God and of His grace. So they do in our case also. When any trouble falls upon us, for any reason,--and there are many reasons other than His anger why God sends trouble upon us,--conscience is up immediately with her interpretation and explanation of our troubles. This is your wages now, conscience says. God has been slow to wrath, but His patience is exhausted now. As Rutherford says in another letter, our tearful eyes look asquint at Christ and He appears to be angry, when all the time He pities and loves us. Is there any man here to-night whose apprehensions are working upon his cross? Is there any man of God here who has lost hold of God in the thick darkness, and who fears that his cross has come to him because God is angry with him? Let him hear and imitate what Rutherford says when in the same distress: 'I will lay inhibitions on my apprehensions,' he says; 'I will not let my unbelieving thoughts slander Christ. Let them say to me "there is no hope," yet I will die saying, It is not so; I shall yet see the salvation of God. I will die if it must be so, under water, but I will die gripping at Christ. Let me go to hell, I will go to hell believing in and loving Christ.' Rutherford's worst apprehensions, his best-grounded apprehensions, could not survive an assault of faith like that. Imitate him, and improve upon him, and say, that with a thousand times worse apprehensions than ever Rutherford could have, yet, like him, you will make your bed in hell, loving, and adoring, and justifying Jesus Christ. And, if you do that, hell will have none of you; all hell will cast you out, and all heaven will rise up and carry you in.

'Challenges' is another of Rutherford's technical terms that he constantly uses to his expert correspondents. 'I was under great challenges,' he says, in this same letter; and in a letter written the same month of March to William Rigg, of Athernie, he says, 'Old challenges revive, and cast all down.' Dr. Andrew Bonar, Rutherford's expert editor, gives this glossary upon these passages: 'Charges, self-upbraidings, self-accusations.' Challenges of conscience came to Rutherford like these: 'Why art thou writing letters of counsel to other men? Counsel thyself first. Why art thou appealed to and trusted and loved by God's best people in Scotland, when thou knowest that thou art a Cain in malice and a Judas in treachery, all but the outbreaks? Why art thou taking thy cross so easily, when thou knowest the unsettled controversy the Lord still has with thee?' 'Hall binks are slippery,' wrote stern old Knockbrex, challenging his old minister for his too great joy. 'Old challenges now and then revive and cast all down again.' That reminds me of a fine passage in that great book of Rutherford's, *Christ Dying*, where he shows us how to take out a new charter for all our possessions, and for the salvation of our souls themselves when our salvation, or our possessions and our right to them, is challenged. It is better, he says, to hold your souls and your lands by prayer than by obedience, or conquest, or industry. Have you wisdom, honour, learning, parts, eloquence, godliness, grace, a good name, wife, children, a house, peace, ease, pleasure? Challenge yourself how you got them, and see that you hold them by an unchallengeable charter, even by prayer, and then by grace. And if you hold these things by any other charter, hasten to get a new conveyance made and a new title drawn out. And thus old, and angry, and threatening challenges will work out a charter that cannot be challenged.

And, then, when George Gillespie was lying on his deathbed in Edinburgh, with his pillow filled with stinging apprehensions, as is often the case with God's best servants and ripest saints, hear how his old friend, now professor of divinity in St. Andrews, writes to him:--

'My reverend and dear brother, look to the east. Die well. Your life of faith is just finishing. Finish it well. Let your last act of faith be your best act. Stand not upon sanctification, but upon justification. Hand all your accounts over to free grace. And if you have any bands of apprehension in your death, recollect that your apprehensions are not canonical.' And the dying man answered: 'There is nothing that I have done that can stand the touchstone of God's justice. Christ is my all, and I am nothing.'

# XIX.  JOHN FERGUSHILL

'Ho, ye that have no money, come and buy in the poor man's
market.'-- **Rutherford**.

It makes us think when we find two such men as Samuel Rutherford and John
Fergushill falling back for their own souls on a Scripture like this.  We naturally think of Scriptures like this as specially sent out to the chief of sinners; to
those men who have sold themselves for naught, or, at least, to new beginners
in the divine life.  We do not readily think of great divines and famous preachers
like Rutherford, or of godly and able pastors like Fergushill, as at all either need-
ing such Scriptures as this, or as finding their own case at all met in them.  But it is
surely a great lesson to us all--a great encouragement and a great rebuke--to find
two such saintly men as the ministers of Anwoth and Ochiltree reassuring and
heartening one another about the poor man's market as they do in their letters to
one another.  And their case is just another illustration of this quite familiar fact in
the Church of Christ, that the preachers who press their pulpits deepest into the
doctrines of grace, and who, at the same time, themselves make the greatest attainments in the life of grace, are just the men, far more than any of their hearers,
both to need and to accept the simplest, plainest, freest, fullest offer of the Gospel.
If the men of the house of Israel will not accept the peace you preach to them, said
our Lord to His first apostles, then take that peace home to yourselves.  And how
often has that been repeated in the preaching of the Gospel since the days of Peter
and John! How often have our best preachers preached their best sermons to themselves!  'I preached the following Lord's Day,' says Boston in his diary, 'on "Why
art thou cast down, O my soul?" and my sermon was mostly on my own account.'
And it was just because Boston preached so often in that egoistical way that the

people of Ettrick were able to give such a good account of what they heard. Weep yourselves, if you would have your readers weep, said the shrewd old Roman poet to the shallow poetasters of his Augustan day. And the reproof and the instruction come up from every pew to every pulpit still. 'Feel what you say, if you would have us feel it. Believe what you say, if you would have us believe it. Flee to the refuge yourselves, if you would have us flee. And let us see you selling all in the poor man's market, if you would see us also selling all and coming after you.' The people of Anwoth and Ochiltree were very well off in this respect also that their ministers did not bid them do anything that they did not first do themselves. The truest and best apostolical succession had come to those two parishes in that their two pastors were able, with a good conscience before God and before their people, to say with Paul to the Philippians: 'Those things, which ye have both learned, and received, and heard, and seen in me do; and the God of peace shall be with you.'

As to the merchandise of the poor man's market,--that embraces everything that any man can possibly need or find any use for either in this world or in the next. Absolutely everything is found in the poor man's market--everything, from God Himself, the most precious of all things, down to the sinner himself, the most vile and worthless of all things. The whole world, and all the worlds, are continually thrown into this market, both by the seller and by the purchaser. The seller holds nothing back from this market, and the purchaser comes to this market for everything. Even what he already possesses; even what he bought and paid for but yesterday; even what everybody else would call absolutely the poor man's own, he throws it all back again upon God every day, and thus holds all he has as his instant purchase of the great Merchantman. The poor man's market is as far as possible from being a Vanity Fair, but the catalogues and the sale-lists of that fair may be taken as a specimen of the things that change hands continually in the poor man's market also. For here also are sold such merchandise as houses, lands, trades, places, honours, preferments, pleasures and delights of all sorts; wives, husbands, children, masters, servants, lives, blood, bodies, souls, gold, silver, and what not. All these things God sells to poor men every day; and for all these things, as often as they need any of them, His poor men come to His market for them. And, as has been said, even after they have got possession of any or all of these things, as if the market had an absolute fascination for them, like gamblers who cannot stay away from the wheel, they are back again, buying and selling what, but yesterday, they took home with them as the best bargain they had ever made. Yes, the things that, once possessed, either by inheritance or by purchase or by gift, you would think they would die rather than part with--a patrimony in ancient lands and houses, a possession they had toiled and prayed and waited for all their days, Christ on His cross, their own child in his cradle--absolutely everything they possess, or would die to possess, they part with again, just that they may have the excitement, the debate, the delight, the security, and the liberty of purchasing it all over again every day in the poor man's market.

Over all this merchandise God Himself is the Master Merchant. It all belongs to Him, and He has put it all into the poor man's purchase. He owns all the merchandise, and He has opened the market: He invites and advertises the purchasers, fixes the prices, and settles the conditions of sale. And the first condition of sale is that all intending purchasers shall come to Himself immediately for whatever they need. All negotiation here must be held immediately with God. There are no middlemen here. They have their own place in the markets of earth; but there is no room and no need for them here. The producer and the purchaser meet immediately here. He employs whole armies of servants to distribute and deliver His goods, but the bargain itself must be struck with God alone. The price must be paid directly to Him; and then, with His own hand, He will write out your right and title to your purchase. Let every poor man, then, be sure to draw near to God, and to God alone. Draw near to God, and He will draw near to you. Ho, ye that have no money: incline your ear, and come to Me: hear, and your soul shall live!

Now, surely, one of the most remarkable things about the purchasers in this market is just their fewness. We find Isaiah in his day canvassing the whole of Jerusalem, high and low, and glad to get even one purchaser here and another there. And Rutherford, looking back to Anwoth from Aberdeen, was not sure that he had got even so much as one really earnest purchaser brought near to God. And thus it was that, while at Anwoth, he was so much in that market himself. Partly on the principle that preachers are bidden to take to themselves for their trouble what their proud people refuse, and partly because Rutherford was out of all sight the poorest man in all Anwoth.

Now, what made Isaiah and Rutherford and Fergushill such poor men themselves, was just this, that they came out of every money-making enterprise in the divine life far poorer men than they entered it. There are some unlucky men in life who never prosper in anything. Everything goes against them. Everything makes shipwreck into which they adventure their time and their money and their hope. They go into one promising concern after another with flying colours and a light heart. Other men have made great fortunes here, and so will they; but before long their old evil luck has overtaken them, and they are glad that they are not all their life in prison for the uttermost farthing. And so on, till at last they have to go to the poor man's market for the last decencies of their death and burial; for their winding-sheet, and their coffin, and their grave. And so was it with the ministers of Anwoth and Ochiltree; and so it is with all that poverty-stricken class of ministers to which they belonged. For, whatever their attainments and performances in preaching or in pastoral work may do to enrich others, one thing is certain: all they do only impoverishes to pennilessness the men who put their whole life and their whole heart into the performance of such work. Their whole service of God, both in the public ministry of the word, and in their more personal submission to His law, has this fatal and hopeless principle ruling it, that the better it is done, and the more completely any man gives himself up to the doing of it, the poorer and the weaker it leaves him who does it. So much so, that while he leads other men into the way of the greatest riches, he himself sinks deeper and deeper into poverty of spirit every day. Till, out of sheer pity, and almost remorse, that His service should entail such poverty on all His servants, Christ sends them out continually less with an invitation to their people than to themselves, saying always to them, 'Take the invitation to yourselves; and he of My servants who hath no money let him buy without money and bear away what he will.' 'My dear Fergushill, our Lord is not so cruel as to let a poor man see salvation and never let him touch it for want of money; indeed, the only thing that commendeth sinners to Christ is their extreme necessity and want. Ho, he that hath no money, that is the poor man's market.' When James Guthrie was lying ill and like to die, he called in his man, James Cowie, to read in the Epistle to the Romans to him, and when Cowie came to these words, 'I will have mercy on whom I will have mercy,' his master burst into tears, and said, 'James, I have nothing but that to lippen to.'

Look now at the prices that are demanded and paid in the poor man's market.

And, paradoxical and past all understanding as are so many of the things connected with this matter, the most paradoxical and past all understanding of them all is the price that is always asked, and that is sometimes paid, in that market. When any man comes here to buy, it is not the value of the article on sale that is asked of him; but the first question that is asked of him is, How much money have you got? And if it turns out that he is rich and increased with goods, then, to him, the price, even of admittance to this market, is all that he has. The very entrance-money, before he comes in sight of the stalls and tables at all, has already stripped him bare of every penny he possesses. And that is why so few purchasers are found in this market; they do not feel able or willing to pay down the impoverishing entrance-price. As a matter of fact, it is a very unusual thing to find a young man who has been so well taught about this market by his parents, his schoolmasters, or even by his ministers, that he is fit to enter early on its great transactions. And increasing years do not tend of themselves to reconcile him to the terms on which God sells His salvation. The price in the poor man's market is absolutely everything that a rich man possesses; and then, when he has nothing left, when he has laid down all that he has, or has lost all, or has been robbed of all, only then the full paradox of the case comes into his view; for then he begins to discover that the price he could not meet or face so long as he was a rich and a well-to-do man is such a price that, in his absolute penury, he can now pay it down till all the market is his own. Multitudes of poor men up and down the land remember well, and will never forget, this poor man Rutherford's so Isaiah-like words, 'Our wants best qualify us for Christ'; and again, 'All my own stock of Christ is some hunger for Him.' 'Say Amen to the promises, and Christ is yours,' he wrote to Lady Kenmure. 'This is surely an easy market. You need but to look to Him in faith; for Christ suffered for all sin, and paid the price of all the promises.'

'Faith cannot be so difficult, surely,' says William Guthrie in his ***Saving Interest***, 'when it consists of so much in ***desire***.' Now, both its exceeding difficulty and its exceeding ease also just consist in that. Nothing is so easy to a healthy man as the desire for food; but, then, nothing is so impossible to a dead man, or even to a sick man, as just desire. Desire sounds easy, but how few among us have that capacity and that preparation for Christ and His salvation that stands in desire. Have you that desire? Really and truly, in your heart of hearts, have you that desire? Then how well it is with you! For that is all that God looks for in him who comes to the poor man's market; indeed, it is the only currency accepted there. Isaiah's famous invitation is drawn out just to meet the case of a man who has desire, and nothing but desire, in his heart. All the encouragements and assurances that his evangelical genius can devise are set forth by the prophet to attract and to win the desiring heart. The desiring heart says to itself, I would give the whole world if I had it just to see Christ, just to be near Christ, and just, if it were but possible, that I should ever be the least thing like Christ. Now, that carries God. God, the Father of our Lord Jesus Christ, cannot resist that. No true father could, and least of all a father who loves his son, and who has such a son to love as God has in Christ. Well, He says; if you love and desire, honour and estimate My Son like that, I cannot deny Him the reward and the pleasure of possessing you and your love. And thus, without any desert in you--any desert but sheer desire--you have made the greatest, the easiest, the speediest, the most splendid purchase that all the poor man's market affords. No, William Guthrie; faith is not so very difficult to the sinner who has desire. For where desire of the right quality is, and the right quantity, there is everything. And all the merchandise of God is at that sinner's nod and bid.

Ho, then, he that hath no money, but only the *desire* for money, and for what money can, and for what money cannot, buy, come and buy, without money and without price. Instead of money, instead of merit, even if you have nothing but Rutherford's only fitness for Christ, 'My loathsome wretchedness,' then come with that. Come boldly with that. Come as if you had in and on you the complete opposite of that. The opposite of loathsomeness is delightsomeness; and the opposite of wretchedness is happiness. Yes! but you will search all the Book of God and all its promises, and you will not find one single letter of them all addressed to the abounding and the gladsome and the self-satisfied. It is the poor man's market; and this market goes best when the poor man is not only poor, but poor beyond all ordinary poverty: poor, as Samuel Rutherford always was, to 'absolute and loathsome wretchedness.' Let him here, then, whose sad case is best described in Rutherford's dreadful words, let him come to Rutherford's market and make Rutherford's merchandise, and let him do it now. Ho, he that hath no money, he that hath only misery, let him come, and let him come now.

# XX.  JAMES BAUTIE, STUDENT OF DIVINITY

'You crave my mind.'-- *Rutherford*.

As a rule the difficulties of a divinity student are not at all the difficulties of the best of his future people.  A divinity student's difficulties are usually academic and speculative, whereas the difficulties of the best people in his coming congregation will be difficulties of the most intensely real and practical kind.  And thus it is that we so often hear lately-ordained ministers confessing that they have come to the end of their resources and experiences, and have nothing either fresh or certain left to preach to the people about.  Just as, on the other hand, so many congregations complain that they look up to the pulpit from Sabbath to Sabbath and are not fed.  It is not much to be wondered at that a raw college youth cannot all at once feed and guide and extricate an old saint; or that a minister, whose deepest difficulties hitherto have been mostly of the debating society kind, should not be able to afford much help to those of his people who are wading through the deep and drowning waters of the spiritual life.  And whether something could not be done by the institution of chairs of genuine pastoral and experimental theology for the help of our students and the good of our people is surely a question that well deserves the earnest attention of all the evangelical churches.  Meantime we are to be introduced to a divinity student of the middle of the seventeenth century who was early and deeply exercised in those intensely real problems of the soul which occupied such a large place both in the best religious literature and in the best pulpit work of that intensely earnest day. James Bautie, or Beattie, as we shall here call him on Dr. Bonar's suggestion, was a candidate for the ministry such that the ripest and most deeply exercised saints in Scotland might well have rejoiced to have had such an able and saintly youth for their preacher on the

Sabbath-day as well as for their pastor all the week. As James Beattie's college days drew on to an end he became more and more exercised about his mental deficiencies, and still more about his spiritual unfitness to be anybody's minister. Beattie had, to begin with, this always infallible mark of an able man--an increasing sense of his own inability: and he had, along with that, this equally infallible mark of a spiritually-minded man--an overwhelming sense of his utter lack of anything like a spiritual mind. No man but a very able man could have written the letter that Beattie wrote about himself to Samuel Rutherford; and Rutherford's letter back to Beattie will not be a bad test of a divinity student whether he has enough of the true divinity student mind in him to read that letter, to understand it, and to translate it. Beattie had an excellent intellect, and his excellent intellect had not been laid out at college on those windy fields that so puff up a beginner in knowledge and in life; his whole mind had been given up already to those terrible problems of the soul that both humble and exalt the man who spends his life among them. Beattie's future congregation will not vaunt themselves about their minister's ability or scholarship or eloquence; his sermons will soon push his people back behind all such superficial matters. Beattie's preaching and his whole pastorate will soon become another illustration of the truth that it is not gifts but graces in a minister that will in the long-run truly edify the body of Christ. You have James Beattie's portrait as a divinity student in Rutherford's 249th letter, and you will find a complementary portrait of Beattie as a grey-haired pastor in Dr. Stalker's *Preacher and his Models*. 'He was a man of competent scholarship, and had the reputation of having been in early life a powerful and popular preacher. But it was not to those gifts that he owed his unique influence. He moved through the town, with his white hair and somewhat staid and dignified demeanour, as a hallowing presence. His very passing in the street was a kind of benediction; the people, as they looked after him, spoke of him to each other with affectionate reverence. Children were proud when he laid his hand on their heads, and they treasured the kindly words which he spoke to them. They who laboured along with him in the ministry felt that his mere existence in the community was an irresistible demonstration of Christianity and a tower of strength to every good cause. Yet he had not gained this position of influence by brilliant talents or great achievements or the pushing of ambition; for he was singularly modest, and would have been the last to credit himself with half the good he did. The whole mystery lay in this, that he had lived in the town for forty years a blameless life, and was known by everybody to be a godly and a prayerful man. The prime qualification for the ministry is goodness.'

Beattie as a student challenged himself severely on this account also, that some truths found a more easy and unshaken credit with him than other truths. This is a common difficulty with many of our modern students also, and how best to advise with them under this real difficulty constantly puts their professors and their pastors to the test. Whatever Beattie may have got, I confess I do not get much help in this difficulty out of Rutherford's letter back to Beattie. Rutherford, with all his splendid gifts of mind and heart, had sometimes a certain dogmatic and dictatorial way with him, and this is just the temper that our students still meet with too often in their old and settled censors. The 'torpor of assurance' has not yet settled on the young divine as it has done on too many of the old. There was a modest, a genuine, and an every way reasonable difficulty in this part of Beattie's letter to Rutherford, and I wish much that Rutherford had felt himself put upon his quite capable mettle to deal with the difficulty. Or, if he had not time to go to the bottom of all Beattie's deep letter, as he says he has not, he might have referred his correspondent--for his correspondent was a well-read student--to a great sermon by the greatest of English Churchmen--a sermon that a reader like Rutherford must surely have had by heart, entitled, 'A Learned and Comfortable Sermon of the Certainty and Perpetuity of Faith in the Elect.' But, unfortunately for England and Scotland both, England was thrusting that sermon and all the other writings of its author on the Church of Christ in Scotland at the point of the bayonet, and that is the very worst instrument that can be employed in the interests of truth and of ecclesiastical comprehension and conformity. And among the many things we have to be thankful for in our more emancipated and more catholic day, it is not the least that Rutherford and Hooker lie in peace and in complemental fulness beside one another on the tables of all our students of divinity.

Coming still closer home to himself, our divinity student puts this acute difficulty to his spiritual casuist: Whether a man of God, and especially a minister of Christ, can be right who does not love God for Himself, for His nature and for His character solely and purely, and apart altogether from all His benefactions both in nature and in grace. James Beattie had been brought up with such a love for the

Kirk of Scotland, and for her ministers and her people; he had of late grown into such a love for his books also, and for the work of the ministry, that in examining himself in prospect of his approaching licence he had felt afraid that he loved the thought of a study, and a pulpit, and a manse, and its inhabitants, and, indeed, the whole prospective life of a minister, with more keenness of affection than he loved the souls of men, or even his Master Himself. And he put that most distressing difficulty also before Rutherford. Now there was an expression on that matter that was common in the pulpits of Rutherford's school in that day that Rutherford would be sure to quote in his second letter to Beattie, if not in his first. It was a Latin proverb, but all the common people of that day quite well understood it, not to speak of a student like Beattie. *Aliquid in Christo formosius Salvatore*, wrote Rutherford to distressed Beattie; that is to say, There is that in Christ which is far more fair and sweet than merely His being a Saviour. Never be content, that is, till you can rise up above manses and pulpits and books and sermons, and even above your own salvation, to see the pure and infinite loveliness of Christ Himself. Dost thou, O my soul, love Jesus Christ for Himself alone, and not only as thy Redeemer? though to love Him as such He doth allow thee, yet there is that in Christ that is far more amiable than merely in His being thy Saviour. And yet the two kinds of love may quite well stand together, writes Rutherford, just as a child loves his mother because she is his mother, and yet his love leaps the more out when she gives him an apple. At the same time, to love Christ for Himself alone is the last end of a true believer's love.

It was one of the great experimental problems much agitated among the greater evangelical divines of that deep, clear-eyed, and honest day, Why the truly regenerate are all left so full of all manner of indwelling sin. We never hear that question raised nowadays, nor any question at all like that. The only difficulty in our day is why any man should have any difficulty about his own indwelling sin at all. But neither Beattie, nor Rutherford, nor any of the masters who remain to us had got so far as we. And as for the Antinomian, perfectionist, and higher-life preachers of that day, they are all so dead and forgotten that you would not know their names even if I repeated them. Beattie, as a beginner in the spiritual life, had made this still not uncommon mistake. He had taken those New Testament passages in which the apostles portray an ideal Christian man as he stands in the election and calling of God, and as he will be found at last and for ever in heaven, and he had prematurely and inconsequently applied all that to himself as a young man under sanctification and under the painful and humiliating beginnings of it; and no wonder that, so confusing the very first principles of the Gospel, he confused and terrified himself out of all peace and all comfort and all hope. Now, that was just the kind of difficulty with which Rutherford could deal with all his evangelical freedom and fulness, depth and insight. No preacher or writer of that day held up the absolute necessity of holiness better than Rutherford did; but then, that only the more compelled him to hold up also such comfort as he conveys in his consoling and reassuring letter to despairing Beattie: 'Comparing the state of one truly regenerate, whose heart is a temple of the Holy Ghost, with your own, which is full of uncleanness and corruption, you stand dumb and dare not call Christ heartsomely your own. But, I answer, the best regenerate have their defilements, and, wash as they will, there will be the filth of sin in their hearts to the end. Glory alone will make our hearts pure and perfect, never till then will they be absolutely sinless.' And if we, Rutherford's so weak-kneed successors, preached the law of God and true holiness as he preached those noble doctrines, the sheer agony of our despairing people would compel us to preach also the true nature, the narrow limits, and the whole profound laws of evangelical sanctification as we never preach, and scarce dare to preach, those things now. They who preach true holiness best are just thereby the more compelled to preach its partial, tentative, elementary, and superficial character in this life. And the hearer who knows in the word of God and in his own heart what indeed true holiness is, will insist on having its complementary truths frequently preached to him to keep him from despair; or else he will turn continually to those great divines who, though dead, yet preach such things in their noble books. And that those books are not still read and preached among us, and that the need for them and their doctrines is so little felt, is only another illustration of the true proverb that where no oxen are the crib is clean.

James Beattie was in very good company when he said that he must have more assurance, both of his gifts and his graces, before he could enter on his ministry. For Moses, and Isaiah, and Jeremiah, and many another minister who could be named, have all felt and said the same thing. Now that he is near the door of the pulpit, Beattie feels that he cannot enter it till he has more certainty that it is all right with himself. But our young ministers will attain to assurance not so much by consulting

Rutherford, skilled casuist in such matters as he is, as by themselves going forward in a holy life and a holy ministry. 'It is not God's design,' says Jonathan Edwards, 'that men should obtain assurance in any other way than by mortifying corruption, increasing in grace, and obtaining the lively exercises of it. Assurance is not to be obtained so much by self-examination as by action. Paul obtained assurance of winning the prize more by running than by reflecting. The swiftness of his pace did more toward his assurance of the goal than the strictness of his self-examination.' 'I wish you a share of my feast,' replies Rutherford. 'But, for you, hang on our Lord, and He will fill you with a sense of His love, as He has so often filled me. Your feast is not far off. Hunger on; for there is food already in your hunger for Christ. Never go away from Him, but continue to fash Him; and if He delays, yet come not away, albeit you should fall aswoon at His feet.' Pray, says Rutherford, and you will not long lack assurance. Work, says Edwards, and assurance of God's love will be an immediate earnest of your full wages.

# XXI. JOHN MEINE, JUNR., STUDENT OF DIVINITY

'If you would be a deep divine I recommend you to
sanctification.'-- *Rutherford*.

O ld John Meine's shop was a great howf of Samuel Rutherford's all the
time of his student life in Edinburgh. Young Rutherford had got an
introduction to the Canongate shopkeeper from one of the elders of
Jedburgh, and the old shopkeeper and the young student at once took to
one another, and remained fast friends all their days. John Meine's shop was so sit-
uated at a corner of the Canongate that Rutherford could see the Tolbooth and John
Knox's house as he looked up the street, and Holyrood Palace as he looked down,
and the young divine could never hear enough of what the old shopkeeper had to
tell him of Holyrood and its doings on the one hand, and of the Reformer's house on
the other. The very paving-stones of the Canongate were full of sermons on the one
hand, and of satires on the other, in that day. 'He was an old man when he came to
live near my father's shop,' John Meine would say to the eager student. 'But, even
as an errand boy, taking parcels up his stair, I felt what a good man's house I was in,
and I used to wish I was already a man, that I might either be a soldier or a minister.'
The divinity student often sat in the shopkeeper's pew on Sabbath-days, and after
sermon they never went home till they had again visited John Knox's grave. And
as they turned homeward, old Meine would lay his hand on young Rutherford's
shoulder and say: 'Knoxes will be needed in Edinburgh again, before all is over, and
who knows but you may be elect, my lad, to be one of them?'

Barbara Hamilton, who lived above her husband's shop, was almost more
young Rutherford's intimate friend than even her intimate husband. Barbara Hamilton was both a woman of eminent piety and of a high and bold public spirit. And

stories are still told in the Wodrow Books of her interest and influence in the affairs of the Kirk and its silenced ministers. The godly old couple had two children: John, called after his father, and Barbara, called after her mother, and Barbara assisted her mother in the house, while John ran errands and assisted his father. Rutherford and the little boy had made a great friendship while the latter was still a boy; and one of Rutherford's fellow-students had made a still deeper friendship upstairs than any but the two friends themselves suspected. Twenty years after this Barbara Hume will receive a letter from Samuel Rutherford, written in the Jerusalem Chamber at Westminster, consoling and sanctifying her for the death of his old friend William Hume, lately chaplain in the Covenanters' army at Newcastle.

By the time that Rutherford was minister at Anwoth, and then prisoner in Aberdeen, John Meine, junior, had grown up to be almost a minister himself. He is not yet a minister, but he is now a divinity student, hard at work at his books, and putting on the shopkeeper's apron an hour every afternoon to let his father have a rest. The old merchant used to rise at all hours in the morning, and spend the early summer mornings on Arthur's Seat with his Psalm-book in his hand, and the winter mornings at his shop fire, reading translations from the Continental Reformers, comparing them with his Bible, singing Psalms by himself and offering prayer. Till his student son felt, as he stood behind the counter for an hour in the afternoon, that he was like Aaron and Hur holding up his father's praying and prevailing hands.

There have always been speculative difficulties and animated debates in our Edinburgh Theological Societies, and, from the nature of the study, from the nature of the human mind, and from the nature of the Scottish mind, there will always be. John Meine's difficulties were not the same difficulties that exercise the minds of the young divines in our day, but they were anxious and troublesome enough to him, and he naturally turned to his old friend at Anwoth for counsel and advice. When Rutherford came in to Edinburgh, there was always a prophet's chamber in Barbara Hamilton's house ready for him; and when the winter session came to a close her young son would set off to Anwoth with a thousand questions in his head. But Aberdeen was too far away, and, though the posts of that day were expensive and uncertain, the old merchant did not grudge to see his son's letters sent off to Samuel Rutherford. Samuel Rutherford knew that John Meine, junior, was not shallow in his divinity, young as he was, nor an entire stranger to sanctification, else he would not have written that still extant letter back to him:--'I have little of Christ in this prison, little but desires. All my present stock of Christ is some hunger for Him; I cannot say but that I am rich in that. But, blessed be my Lord, who taketh me as I am. Christ had only one summer in His year, and shall we insist on two? My love to your father. And, for yourself, if you would be a deep divine, I recommend you to sanctification.' What with his father and his mother, his books, his acquaintance with Rutherford and Hume, and, best of all, his acquaintance with his own evil heart, young John Meine must have been a somewhat deep divine already, else Rutherford would not have cast such pearls of experience down before him.

A divine, according to our division of labour, is a man who has chosen as his life-work to study the things of God; the things, that is, of God in Christ, in Scripture, in the Church, and in the heart and life of man. John and James and Peter and Andrew ceased to be fishermen, and became divines when Christ said to them 'Follow me.' And after seventy years of sanctification the second son of Zebedee had at last attained to divinity enough to receive the Revelation, to write it out, and to be called by the early Church John the Divine.

But what is this process of sanctification that makes a young man already a deep divine? What is sanctification? Rutherford had a deep hand in drawing up the well-known definition, and, therefore, we may take it as not far from the truth: 'Sanctification is the work of God's free grace, whereby we are renewed in the whole man after the image of God, and are enabled more and more to die unto sin and live unto righteousness.' That, or something like that, was the recipe that Samuel Rutherford sent south to John Meine, student of divinity, with the assurance that, if he followed it close enough and long enough, it would result in making him a deep divine. I wonder if he took the recipe; I wonder if he kept to it; I wonder how he pictured to himself the image of God; I wonder, nay, I know, how he felt as he submitted his whole man--body, soul, and spirit--to the renewing of the Holy Ghost. And did he begin and continue to die more and more unto sin, till he died altogether to this sinful world, and live more and more unto righteousness, till he went to live with Knox, and Rutherford, and Hume, and his father and mother in the Land of Life?

'Did he begin with regeneration?' Dr. John Duncan, of the New College, asked his daughter, one Sabbath when she had come home from church full of praise of a sermon she had just heard on sanctification. Dr. Duncan was perhaps the deepest divine this century has seen in Edinburgh; and his divinity took its depth from the same study and the same exercise that Rutherford recommended to John Meine. Dr. Duncan was a great scholar, but it was not his scholarship that made him such a singularly deep divine. He was a profound philosopher also; but neither was it his philosophy. He was an immense reader also; but neither was it the piles of books; it was, he tells us, first the new heart that he got as a student in Aberdeen, and then it was the lifelong conflict that went on within him between the old heart and the new. And it is this that makes sanctification rank and stand out as the first and the oldest of all the experimental sciences. Long before either of the Bacons were born, the humblest and most obscure of God's saints were working out their own salvation on the most approved scientific principles and methods. Long before science and philosophy had discovered and set their seal to that method, the Church of Christ had taught it to all her true children, and all her best divines had taken a deep degree by means of it. What experimentalists were David and Asaph and Isaiah and Paul; and that, as the subtlest and deepest sciences must be pursued, not upon foreign substances but upon themselves, upon their own heart, and mind, and will, and disposition, and conversation, and character. Aristotle says that 'Young men cannot possess practical judgment, because practical judgment is employed upon individual facts, and these are learned only by experience, and a youth has not experience, for experience is gained only by a course of years.'

'A truly great divine,' was Jonathan Edwards' splendid certificate to our own Thomas Boston. Now, when we read his *Memoirs*, written by himself, we soon see what it was that made Boston such a truly great and deep divine. It was not the number of his books, for he tells us how he was pained when a brother minister opened his book-press and smiled at its few shelves. 'I may be a great bookman,' writes Rutherford to Lady Kenmure, 'and yet be a stark idiot in the things of Christ.' It was not his knowledge of Hebrew, though he almost discovered that hidden language in Ettrick. No, but it was his discovery of himself, and his experimental study of his own heart. 'My duties, the best of them, would damn me; they must all be washed with myself in that precious blood. Though I cannot be free of sin, God Himself knows that He would be welcome to make havoc of all my lusts to-night, and to make me holy. I know no lust I would not be content to part with to-night.

The first impression on my spirit this morning was my utter inability to put away sin. I saw that it was as possible for a rock to raise itself as it was for me to raise my heart from sin to holiness.'

But the study of divinity is not a close profession: a profession for men only, and from which women are shut out; nor is the method of it shut off from any woman or any man. 'I counsel you to study sanctification,' wrote Rutherford, the same year to the Lady Cardoness. And if you think that Rutherford was a closet mystic and an unpractical and head-carried enthusiast, too good for this rough world, read his letter to Lady Cardoness, and confess your ignorance of this great and good man. 'Deal kindly with your tenants,' he writes, 'and let your conscience be your factor'; and again, 'When your husband's passion overcomes him, my counsel to your lady-ship is, that a soft answer putteth away wrath.' And lastly, 'Let it not be said that the Lord hath forsaken your house because of your neglect of the Sabbath-day and its exercises. I counsel you to study sanctification among your tenants, and beside your husband, and among your children and your guests. Your lawful and loving pastor, in his only, only Lord,--SAMUEL RUTHERFORD.

## XXII.  ALEXANDER BRODIE OF BRODIE

'Mr. Rutherford's letter desiring me to deny myself.'
--Brodie's **Diary**.

Alexander Brodie was born at Brodie in the north country in the year 1617.  That was the same year that saw Samuel Rutherford matriculate in the College of Edinburgh.  Of young Brodie's early days we know nothing; for, though he has left behind him a full and faithful diary both of his personal and family life, yet, unfortunately, Brodie did not begin to keep that diary till he was well advanced in middle age.  Young Brodie's father died when his son and heir was but fourteen years old, and after taking part of the curriculum of study in King's College, Aberdeen, the young laird married a year before he had come to his majority.  His excellent wife was only spared to be with him for two years when she was taken away from him, leaving him the widowed father of one son and one daughter.

As time goes on we find the laird of Brodie a member of Parliament, a member of General Assembly, and a Lord of Session.  He was one of the commissioners also, who were sent out to the Hague to carry on negotiations with Charles, and during the many troubled years that followed that mission, we find Brodie corresponding from time to time with Cromwell and his officers, and with Charles and his courtiers, both about public and private affairs.  Brodie was one of the ablest men of his day in Scotland, and he should have stood in the very front rank of her statesmen and her saints; but, as it is, he falls very far short of that.  We search the signatures of the National Covenant in vain for the name of Alexander Brodie, and the absence of his name from that noble roll is already an ill-omen for his future life.  David Laing, in his excellent preface to Brodie's **Diary**, is good enough to set down the absence of Brodie's name from the Covenant to his youth and retired habits. I wish I could take his editor's lenient view of Brodie's absence from Greyfriars church on the testing day of the Covenant. It would be an immense relief to me if I could persuade myself to look at Brodie in that matter with Mr. Laing's eyes. I have tried hard to do so, but I cannot. Far younger men than the laird of Brodie were in the Greyfriars churchyard that day, and far more modest men than he was. And I cannot shut my eyes to what appears to me, after carefully studying his life and his character, a far likelier if a far less creditable reason. After the Restoration Brodie's life, if life it could be called, was spent in a constant terror lest he should lose his estates, his liberty, and his life in the prelatic persecution; but, with his sleepless management of men, if not with the blessing of God and the peace of a good conscience, Alexander Brodie died in his own bed, in Brodie Castle, on the 17th of April, 1680.

There were some things in which Alexander Brodie ran well, to employ the apostle's expression; in some things, indeed, no man of his day ran better. To begin with, Brodie had an excellent intellect. If he did not always run well it was not for want of a sound head or a sharp eye. In reading Brodie's diary you all along feel that you are under the hand of a very able man, and a man who all his days does excellent justice to his excellent mind, at least on its intellectual side. The books he enters as having read on such and such a date, the catalogues of books he buys on his visits to Edinburgh and London, and the high planes of thought on which his mind dwells when he is at his best, all bespeak a very able man doing full justice to his great ability. The very examinations he puts himself under as to his motives and mainsprings in this and that action of his life; the defences and exculpations he puts forward for this and that part of his indefensible conduct; the debate he holds now with the presbyterian party and now with the prelatist; the very way he puts his finger down on the weak and unsound places in both of the opposing parties; and, not least, his power of aphoristic thought and expression in the running diary of his spiritual life, all combine to leave the conviction on his reader's mind that Lord Brodie was one of the very ablest men of a very able day in Scotland. I open his voluminous diary at random, and I at once come on such passages as these: 'If substantial duties are neglected or slighted it is a shrewd suspicion, be the repentance what it will, that all is not right. Lord, discover Thyself in the duties of the time, and in every substantial duty. At the same time, hang not the weight of our wellbeing on our duties, but on Christ by faith. I am a reeling, unstable, staggering, unsettled, lukewarm creature. For Thy compassion's sake forgive and heal, warm, establish, enlighten, draw me and I will follow. I am full of self-love, darkness in my judgment, fear to confess Thee, or hazard myself, or my estate, or my peace. . . . We poor creatures are commanded by our affections and our passions; they are not at our command; but the Holy One doth exercise all His attributes at His own will; they are all at His command; they are not passions or perturbations in His mind, though they transport us. When I would hate, I cannot. When I would love, I cannot. When I would grieve, I cannot. When I would desire, I cannot. But it is the better for us that all is as He wills. . . . Another of the deep deceits of my heart is this, that I have more affection in prayer than I have corresponding holiness in my walk or conversation. I wondered not to see the men of the world so taken up with covetous, ambitious, vain projects, for no man's head and heart can be so full of them as my head and heart are. Oh keep me from these unsober, distempered, mad, unruly thoughts! When I am away from Thee then I am quite out of my wit. But God can make use of poison to expel poison. Oh, if I were examined and brought to the light, what a monstrous creature I would be seen to be! For as I see myself I am no better than a devil, void of sincerity and of uprightness in what I do myself, and yet judge others, condemning in another man what I excuse and even approve in myself: plunged in deep snares of self-love, not loving others nor judging nor acting for others as I do for myself and for my relations.' And then a passage which might have been taken from *The Confessions* itself: 'Ere I come to glory and to my journey's end, I shall have spent so much of Thy free grace--what in pardoning, what in preventing, what in convincing, what in enlightening, what in strengthening, and confirming, and upholding; what in watering and making me to grow; what in growth of sanctification, knowledge, faith, experience, patience, mortification, uprightness, steadfastness, watchfulness, humiliation, resolution, and self-denial; what for public, what for private, and what for the family; what against snares on the right hand and on the left;--O Lord, the all-sufficiency of Thy grace!' Surely the man must run well and must make a good goal at last who can write about sin and grace in himself in that fashion! And that is not all he wrote on that subject and in that style. You have no idea of the wealth of personal and experimental matter there lies buried in Alexander Brodie's diary. When I first read Brodie's big diary

I said to myself, What a treasure is this I have stumbled upon! Here is yet another of Scotland's statesmen, scholars, and eminent saints. Here, I thought, is an author on the inward life to be set beside Brae and Halyburton, if not beside Shepard and Edwards themselves.

In the religious upbringing also, and lifelong care of his orphaned son and daughter, Brodie was all we could wish to see. In the sanctification and wise occupation of the Sabbath-day; in the family preparation for communion seasons; in the personal and private covenants he encouraged his children to make with God in their own religious life; in the company he brought to his house and to his table; in his own devotional habits at home--in all these all-important matters Brodie was all that a father of children too early bereft of their mother ought to be. Till we do not wonder to find his son commencing his diary on the day of his father's death in this way: 'My precious, worthy, and dear father! I can hardly apprehend the consequence of it to the land, and the Church, and his family. The Lord give instruction. I have seen the godly conversation, holy and Christian walk of a father, his watchfulness and fruitfulness, his secret communion with God, and yet I cannot say that my heart has been won to God by his example.' A complete directory, indeed, for a Highland gentleman's household religion might easily be collected out of Alexander Brodie's domestic diary.

Another thing that greatly drew me to Brodie when I first read his diary was his noble and truly Christian acknowledgment of God in all the manifold experiences and events of his daily life. '23 *rd July*, 1661.--Came through the fells in England to Alsbori and dined there, saw a country full of grass, plentiful in comparison of us, and acknowledged God in it. . . . Thus I saw a large beautiful country, not straitened with the poverty that my native soil labours under. I desired to consider and understand this. . . . I saw a mighty city, London, numerous, many souls in it, great plenty of things, and thought him a great king that had so many things at his command; yet how much greater is He who hath at His command all things created in heaven and on earth. Who shall not fear Him? . . . *August* 17.--Went this afternoon with Cassilis to the Bridge for natural refreshment, and I saw this populous city, and plenty in it. I therein saw something of the Lord's providence, who hath divided the kingdoms of the earth and given them their habitations, not all alike, but as His wisdom hath seen fit. I saw the copper-works also, and acknowledged the Lord in the gifts and the faculties He hath given to the children of men. 27.--I did see the Lord Mayor, his solemnities, and desired to be instructed by what I saw. The variety of the Lord's creatures on other parts of the earth was represented. In this I did acknowledge Him. But all the glory of the city neither abides nor can make its owner any the happier. It cannot be laid hold upon. It is not solid; it is but in conceit. Oh learn me to be crucified to all this and the like, and make me wise unto salvation! *Nov*. 9--Dined at Billingsgate; saw the prison of King's Bench at Southwark, and the workers of glass, in all which I saw the manifold wisdom of God in all the gifts and faculties He hath given to the sons of men. But alas! I am so barren of any thoughts of God, and so have I found myself this day and at all times.'

'Yet, all these fences, and their whole array,
One cunning bosom sin blows quite away.'

Now, there is no more cunning bosom sin in some men than the sin of covetousness, and that sin in Alexander Brodie's heart and life blew almost, if not altogether, away all these and many more fences of his salvation. Well as David Laing edits Alexander Brodie's **Diary**, unfortunately for some of his readers he leaves his index an index of names only, neglecting things. And thus I have had to extemporise an index for myself under such sad heads as those of Brodie's 'passionateness,' his 'covetousness,' his 'time-serving' and 'tuft-hunting,' and suchlike. And I am compelled in truth to say that the entries in my index under 'covetousness' and under 'time-serving' and 'tergiversation' is a long and yet far from exhaustive list. And now, acting, I hope, on the Scriptural principle that

'The saints are lowered that the world may rise,'

I shall say a single word on each of Brodie's two so besetting sins. And, doing in the matter of Brodie's vices as I have just done in the matter of his virtues, I shall let the singularly honest Diarist speak for himself. I certainly would not dare, on any evidence, to characterise or condemn a man like Brodie as he will now characterise and condemn himself. '*July* 30, 1653.--I find covetousness getting deeper and deeper into my heart, insatiable desires of lands and riches, the desire of acquiring my neighbour's property, and many vain projects and want of contentment, albeit I have already what might satisfy and well content me. I find that it is not ten hundred times what I possess that would content and stay my mind from greedy lusts and insatiable desires. What avails prayer as long as these lusts remain? I scarcely allow meat and fish and beer and victual to my family and to the poor. Lord, pity! 21 *Aug*.--Sin and snare are inseparable from this haste to be rich. Lord, in this Thou punishest one sin with another, with unrighteousness, oppression, unevenness, uncharitableness, deceit, falsehood, rigour to tenants, straitenedness to the poor. 24 *Sept*.--Read 1 Cor. viii. 14, 15, which did reprove my straitenedness, my coldness, and my parsimony. 19 *July*.--Was taken up inordinately with trash and hagg. Let not the Lord impute it! 9 *Oct*.--My heart challenged me that I could so freely lay out money on books, plenishing, clothes to myself, and was so loth to lay out for the Lord. Oh, what does this presage and witness but that I am of the earth and that my portion is not blessed, but that my goods are rather accursed! 4 *Nov*.--Neil Campbell staid with me. I found my niggardly nature still encroaching upon me, and made my supplication for escape. *July* 1.--Because I have not employed my wealth in charitable uses, therefore does the Lord take other ways more grievous to me to scatter what I have so sinfully kept back.' And so on, alternately scrimping and confessing; filling his pockets with money, and praying that he may be enabled to open them, he goes on till we read such miserably self-deceiving entries as this almost at the end of his doleful diary: 'I purpose, if the Lord would give strength and grace and constancy, and an honest and sound heart, to lay by some money for such uses from time to time, whereof this much shall be a sign and memorial.'

And then, as to his fear of man, his time-serving, and vacillation in the day of difficult duty, hear his own humiliating confessions: '*Jan*. 20, 1662.--My perplexity continues as to whether I shall move now or not, stay or return, hold by Lauderdale, or make use of the Bishop. I desired to reflect on giving titles, speaking fair, and complying. I found Lauderdale changed to me, and I desired to spread this out before God. I went to Sir George Mushet's funeral, where I was looked at, as I thought, like a speckled bird. I apprehend much trouble to myself, my family, and my affairs, from the ill-will of those who govern. May God keep me under the shadow of His wings. *Oct*. 16.--Did see the Bishop, and in my discourse with him did go far in fair words and the like. The 31.--James Urquhart was with me. Oh that I could attain to his steadfastness and firmness! But, alas! I am soon overcome; I soon yield to the least difficulty. The 26.--Duncan Cuming was here, and I desired him to tell the honest men in the south that though I did not come up their length, I hoped they would not stumble at me.' In other words, 'Tell the prisoners in the Bass and in Blackness, and the martyrs of the Grass-market and the Tolbooth, that Lord Brodie is a Presbyterian at heart, and ought to be a Covenanter and a sufferer with his fellows; but that he loves Brodie Castle and a whole skin better than he loves the Covenant and the Covenanters, or even the Surety of the better covenant.' And having despatched his sympathetic message to the honest men in the South, he takes up his pen again to carry on his diary, which he carries on in these actual terms. Believe me, I copy literally and scrupulously from the humiliating book. 'Die Dom.--I find great averseness in myself to suffering. I am afraid to lose life or estate. I hold it a duty not to abandon those honest ministers that have stuck to the Reformation. And if the Lord would strengthen me, I would desire to confess the truth like them. . . . I questioned whether I might not safely use means to decline the cross and to ward off the wrath of the Lords and the Magistrates. Shall I begin to hear Mr. William Falconer? Shall I write to Seaforth and Argyll to ask them to clear and vindicate me? Shall I forbear to hear that honest minister, James Urquhart, for a time, seeing the storm is like to fall on me if I do so? What counsel shall I give my son? Shall I expose myself and my family to danger at this time? What is Thy will? What is my duty?' And then this able and honest hypocrite has the grace to add: 'A grain of sound faith would easily answer all these questions.' I have a sheaf of such passages. It is sickening work to speak and hear such things. But they must sometimes be spoken and heard, if only to afford a reply to Paul's question in the text: 'Ye did run well: what did hinder you?' How well Alexander Brodie ran for a time, and how well he might have run to the end but for those two sins that did so easily beset him--the love of money and the fear of man! But under the arrest and overthrow that those two so mean and so contemptible vices brought on Brodie, we see his spiritual life, or what might have ripened into spiritual life, gradually but surely decaying, even in his diary, till we read this last entry on the day of his death: 'My darkness has not taken an end, nor my confusions.'

Alexander Brodie being long dead yet speaketh with terrible power in every page of his solemnising diary. Young men of Scotland, he says, young statesmen, young senators of the College of Justice, young churchmen, young magistrates, young landlords, and all young men of talent and of influence, sons of the Cavaliers and the Covenanters alike--seek the right and the true, the just and the honourable, in your day; choose it for your part, and take your stand firmly and boldly upon it. Make hazards in order to stand upon it. Read my humbling life, and take warning from me. And when your times are confused and perplexed; when truth and duty are not wholly and commandingly clear; give a good conscience the benefit of the doubt, and suspect the side on which safety and promotion and public praise lie. Pray without ceasing, and then live as you pray. And then my diary shall not have been written and left open among you in vain.

# XXIII. JOHN FLEMING, BAILIE OF LEITH

'I wish that I could satisfy your desire in drawing up and framing for
you a Christian Directory.'-- **Rutherford**.

Samuel Rutherford and John Fleming, Bailie of Leith, were old and fast friends. Away back in the happy days when Rutherford was still a student, and was still haunting the back-shop of old John Meine in the Canongate of Edinburgh, he had formed a fast friendship with the young wood-merchant of Leith. And all the trials and separations of life, instead of deadening their love for one another, or making them forget one another, had only drawn the two men the closer to one another. For when Rutherford's two great troubles came upon him,--first his dismissal from the Latin regency in Edinburgh University, and then his banishment from his pulpit at Anwoth,--John Fleming came forward on both occasions with money, and with letters, and with visits that were even better than money, to the penniless and friendless professor and exiled pastor. 'Sir, I thank you kindly for your care of me and of my brother. I hope it is laid up for you and remembered in heaven.'

Robert M'Ward, the first editor of Rutherford's *Letters*, with all his assiduity, was only able to recover four letters out of the heap of correspondence that had passed between the rich timber-merchant of Leith and the exiled minister, but, those four tell us volumes, both about the intimacy of the two men and about the depth and the worth of the bailie's character. Fleming wrote a letter to Rutherford in the spring of 1637, which must have run in some such terms as these:--'My life is fast ebbing away, and I am not yet begun aright to live. I am in mid-time of my days. I sometimes feel that I am coming near the end of them; and what evil days they have been! My business that my father left me is prosperous. I have a good and kind wife, as you know. My children are not wholly without promise. My place in this town is far too honourable for me, and I have many dear friends among the godly both in Leith and in Edinburgh. But I feel bitterly that I have no business to mix myself among them, and to be counted one of them. For, what with the burdensome affairs of this great seaport, and my own growing business, my days and my nights are like a weaver's shuttle. I intend and I begin well, but another year and another year comes to an end and I am just where I was. I have had some success, by God's blessing, in making money, but I am a bankrupt before Him in my soul. My inward life is a ravelled hesp, and I need guidance and direction if I am ever to come out of this confusion and to come to any good. Protestant and Presbyterian as I am,' he goes on, 'if I could only find a director who would take trouble with me and command me as I take trouble with and command my servants, I vow to you that I would put the reins without reserve into his hands. Will you not take me in hand? You know me of old. We used to talk in dear old John Meine's backshop on week-nights and upstairs on Sabbath nights about these things. And long as it is since we saw much of one another, I feel that you know me out and in, and through and through, as no one else knows me. Tell me, then, what I am to do with myself. I will try to do what you tell me, for I am wearied and worn out with my stagnant and miserable life. Pity me, Mr. Samuel, my honoured and dear friend, for my pirn is almost run out, and I am not near saved.'

'My worthy and dearly beloved brother in the Lord,' replied Rutherford to Fleming, 'I dare not take it upon me to lay down rules and directions for your inner life. I have not the judiciousness, nor the experience, nor the success in the inner life myself that would justify me. And, besides, there is no lack of such Directories as you ask me for. Search the Scriptures. Buy Daniel Rogers, and Richard Greenham, and especially William Perkins. My own wall is too much broken down, my own garden is too much overrun with weeds; I dare not attempt to lay down the law to you. But I will do this since you are so importunate; I will tell you, as you have told me, some of my own mistakes and failings and shipwrecks, and the rocks on which I have foundered may thus, be made to carry a lantern to light your ship safely past them.'

'Fool, said my Muse to me, look in thy heart and write;

and, like Sir Philip Sydney, Samuel Rutherford looked into his own heart, and drew a Directory out of it for the better Christian conduct of his friend John Fleming.

1. Now--would you believe it?--the first thing Samuel Rutherford found his own heart accusing him in before God was, of all things, the way he had wasted his time. Would you believe it that the student who was summer and winter in his study at three o'clock in the morning, and the minister who, as his people boasted, was always preparing his sermons, always visiting his people, always writing books, and always entertaining strangers,--would you believe it that one of his worst consciences was for the bad improvement of his time? What an insatiable thirst for absolute and unearthly perfection God has awakened in the truly gracious heart! Give the truly gracious heart a little godliness and it cries out night and day for more. Give it more, and it straightway demands all. Give it all and it still accuses you that it has literally got none at all. Samuel Rutherford gave all his time and all his strength to his pastoral and his professorial duties, and yet when he looked into his own heart to write a letter to Bailie Fleming out of it, his whole heart condemned him to his face because he had so mismanaged his time, and had not aright redeemed it. 'You complain that your time is fast speeding away, and that you have not even begun to employ it well. So is mine. I give a good part of my time to my business, as you say you do to yours; but, just like you, that leaves me no time to give to God. God forgive me for the way I forget Him and neglect Him all the time that I am bustling about in the things of His house! Let us both begin, and me especially, to give some of God's best earthly gift back to Him again. Let us spare a little of His time that He allows us and bestow it back again upon Himself. He values nothing so much as a little of our allotted time. Let us meditate on Him more, and pray more to Him. Let us throw up ejaculations of prayer to Him more and more while we are at our daily employments; you in the timber-yard, down among the ships, at the desk, and at the Council-table; and I among my books, and among my people, and in my pulpit. These are always golden moments to me, and why they do not multiply themselves into hours and days and years is to me but another proof of my deep depravity. And, John Fleming, sanctify you the Sabbath. As you love and value your immortal soul, sanctify and do not waste and desecrate the Sabbath. Let no man steal from you a single hour of the Sabbath-day. Six days shalt thou la-

bour and do all thy work, but the seventh day is the Sabbath of the Lord thy God.'

2. And again and again in his letters to Fleming Rutherford returns to the sins of the tongue. Rutherford himself was a great sinner by his tongue, and he seems to have taken it for granted that the bailies of Leith were all in the same condemnation. 'Observe your words well,' he writes out of the bitterness of his own heart. 'Make conscience of all your conversations.' Cut off a right hand, pluck out a right eye, says Christ. And I wonder that half of His disciples have not bitten out their offending tongues. What a world of injury and of all kinds of iniquity has the tongue always and everywhere been! In Jerusalem in David's day; and still in Jerusalem in James's day; in Anwoth and Aberdeen and St. Andrews in Rutherford's day; and in Leith in John Fleming's day; and still in all these places in our own day. The tongue can no man tame, and no wonder, for it is set on fire of hell. 'I shall show you,' says Rutherford, 'what I would fain be at myself, howbeit I always come short of my purpose.' Rutherford made many enemies both as a preacher and as a doctrinal and an ecclesiastical controversialist. He was a hot, if not a bad-blooded man himself, and he raised both hot and bad blood in other men. He was a passionate-hearted man, was Rutherford; he would not have been our sainted Samuel Rutherford if he had not had a fast and a high-beating heart. And his passionate heart was not all spent in holy love to Jesus Christ, though much of it was. For the dregs of it, the unholy scum and froth of it, came out too much in his books of debate and in his differences with his own brethren. His high-mettled and almost reckless sense of duty brought him many enemies, and it was his lifelong sanctification to try to treat his enemies aright, and to keep his own heart and tongue and pen clean and sweet towards them. And he divined that among the merchants and magistrates of Leith, anger and malice, rivalry and revenge were not unknown any more than they were among their betters in the Presbytery and the General Assembly. He knew, for Fleming had told him, that his very prosperity and his father's prosperity had procured for Fleming many enemies. The Norway timber trade was not all in the Fleming hands for nothing. The late Council election also had left Fleming many enemies, and his simple duty at the Council-table daily multiplied them. It was quite unaccountable to him how enemies sprang up all around him, and it was well that he had such an open-eyed and much-experienced correspondent as Rutherford was, to whom he could confide such ghastly discoveries, and such terrible

shocks to faith and trust and love. 'Watch well this one thing, Bailie Fleming, even your deep desire for revenge. Be sure that it is in your heart in Leith to seek revenge as well as it is in my heart here in Aberdeen. Watch, as you would the workings of a serpent, the workings of your sore- hurt heart in the matter of its revenges. Watch how the calamities that come on your enemies refresh and revive you. Watch how their prosperity and their happiness depress and darken you. Disentangle the desire for revenge and the delight in it out of the rank thickets of your wicked heart; drag that desire and delight out of its native darkness; know it, name it, and it will be impossible but that you will hate it like death and hell, and yourself on account of it. Do you honestly wish, as you say you do, for direction as to your duty to your many enemies in Leith, and to God and your own soul among them? Then begin with this: watch and find yourself out in your deep desire for revenge, and in your secret satisfaction and delight to hear it and to speak it. Begin with that; and, then, long after that, and as the divine reward of that, you will be enabled to begin to try to love your enemies, to bless them that curse you, to do good to them that hate you, and to pray for them that despitefully use you and persecute you. You need no Directory for these things from me when you have the Sermon on the Mount in your own New Testament.'

3. And, still looking into his own heart and writing straight out of it, Rutherford says to Fleming, 'I have been much challenged in my conscience, and still am, for not referring all I do to God as my last and chiefest end.' Which is just Samuel Rutherford's vivid way of taking home to himself the first question of the Shorter Catechism which he had afterwards such a deep hand in drawing up. I do not know any other author who deals so searchingly with this great subject as that prince among experimental divines, Thomas Shepard, the founder of Yale in New England. His insight is as good as his style is bad. His English is execrable, but his insight is nothing short of divine. 'The pollution of the whole man, and of all his actions,' he says in his *Parable of the Ten Virgins*, 'consists chiefly in his self-seeking, in making ourselves our utmost end. This makes our most glorious actions vile; this stains them all. And so the sanctification of a sinner consists chiefly in making the Lord our utmost end in all that we do. Every man living seeks himself as his last end and chiefest good, and out of this captivity no human power can redeem us. . . . Make this your last and best end--to live to Christ and to do His will. This is your

last end; this is the end of your being born again--nay, of your being redeemed by His blood--that you may live unto Christ.' And in the same author's ***Meditations and Spiritual Experiences***, he says, 'On Sabbath morning I saw that I had a secret eye to my own name in all that I did, and I judged myself to be worthy of death because I was not weaned from all created glory, from all honour and praise, and from the esteem of men. . . . On Sabbath, again, when I came home, I saw into the deep hypocrisy of my own heart, because in my ministry I sought to comfort and quicken the people that the glory might reflect on me as well as on God. . . . On the evening before the sacrament I saw it to be my duty to sequester myself from all other things and to prepare me for the next day. And I saw that I must pitch first on the right end. I saw that mine own ends were to procure honour to myself and not to the Lord. There was some poor little eye in seeking the name and glory of Christ, yet I sought not it only, but my own glory, too. After my Wednesday sermon I saw the pride of my heart acting thus, that when I had done public work my heart would presently look out and inquire whether I had done it well or ill. Hereupon I saw my vileness to be to make men's opinions my rule, and that made me vile in mine own eyes, and that more and more daily.' 'I have been much challenged,' writes Rutherford to Fleming, 'because I do not refer all I do to God as my last end: that I do not eat and drink and sleep and journey and speak and think for God.' And, the fanatic that he is, he seems to think that that is the calling and chief end not only of ministers like himself and Shepard, but of the bailies and timber-merchants of Edinburgh and Leith also.

4. Lastly, in the closing sentences of this inexhaustible letter, Rutherford says to his waiting and attentive correspondent: 'Growth in grace, sir, should be cared for by you above all other things.' And so it should. Literally and absolutely above all other things. Above good health, above good name, above wealth, and station, and honour. These things, take them all together, if need be, are to be counted loss in order to gain growth in grace. But what is growth in grace? It is growth in everything that is truly good; but Fleming, as he read his Directory daily, would always think of growth in grace as the right improvement of his remaining time, and, especially, its religious use and dedication to God; as also of the government of his own untamed tongue; the extinction of the desire for revenge, and of all delight in the injury of his enemies; and, above all, and including all, in making God his chief

end in all that he did. How all-important, then, is a sound and Scriptural Directory to instruct us how we are to grow in grace. And how precious must that directory-letter have been to a man in dead earnest like John Fleming. It was precious to his heart, you may be sure, above all his ships, and all his woodyards, and all his fine houses, and all his seats of honour. And if his growth in grace in Leith has now become full-grown glory in Heaven, how does he there bless God to-day that ever he met with Samuel Rutherford in old John Maine's shop in his youth, and had him for a friend and a director all his after-days. And when John Fleming at the table above forgets not all His benefits, high up, you may be very sure, among them all he never forgets to put Samuel Rutherford's letters; and, more especially, this very directory-letter we have read here for our own direction and growth in grace this Communion-Sabbath night.

## XXIV.  THE PARISHIONERS OF KILMACOLM

'For want of time I have put you all in one letter.'-- *Rutherford*.

There is a well-known passage in *Lycidas* that exactly describes the religious condition of the parish of Kilmacolm in the year 1639.  For the shepherd of that unhappy sheepfold also had climbed up some other way before he knew how to hold a sheephook, till, week after week, the hungry sheep looked up and were not fed.  The parishioners of Kilmacolm must have been fed to some purpose at one time, for the two letters they write to Rutherford in their present starvation bear abundant witness on every page to the splendid preaching and the skilful pastorate that this parish must at one time have enjoyed.  There must have been men of no common ability, as well as of no common profundity of spiritual life in Kilmacolm during those trying years, for the letters they wrote to Rutherford would have done credit to any of Rutherford's ablest and best correspondents--to William Guthrie, or David Dickson, or Robert Blair, or John Livingstone.  Indeed, the expert author of the *Therapeutica* himself would have been put to it to answer fully and satisfactorily those two so acute and so searching letters.  The Kilmacolm people had heard about the famous answers that Samuel Rutherford, now home again in Anwoth, had written both from Anwoth and from Aberdeen to all classes of people and on all kinds of subjects; copies, indeed, of some of those now already widespread letters had come to Kilmacolm itself, till, at one of their private meetings for conference and prayer, it was resolved that a small committee of their elders should gather up their painful experiences in the spiritual life that got no help from the parish pulpit, and should set them by way of submission and consultation before the great spiritual casuist.  Everybody else was getting what counsel and comfort they needed from the famous adviser of Anwoth, and why not they, the neglected parishioners of Kilmacolm? And thus it was that two or three of the oldest and ablest men in the kirk-session so wrote to Rutherford, as, after some delay, to get back the elaborate letter from Anwoth numbered 286 in Dr. Bonar's edition.

I am tempted to think it possible that the old, long-experienced, and much-exercised saints of Kilmacolm may have demanded a little too much of their minister: at any rate, I am quite as anxious to hear what Rutherford shall say to them as they can be to hear from him themselves. And all that leads me to believe that not only must there have been some quite remarkable people in the parish church at that date, but that they must also have had some very special pulpit and pastoral work expended on them in former years. Or, if not that, then their case is just another illustration of what Rutherford says in his reassuring answer, namely, that the life of grace among a people is not at all tied up to the lips of their minister. Which, again, is just another way of putting what the Psalmist says of himself in his humble and happy boast: 'I have more understanding than all my teachers, for Thy testimonies are my meditation. I understand more than the ancients, because I keep Thy precepts.'

1. The first complaint that came to Anwoth from Kilmacolm was expressed in the quaint and graphic language natural to that day. 'Security, strong and sib to nature, is stealing in upon us.' The holy law of God, they mean, was never preached in their parish; at any rate, it was never carried home to any man's conscience. Nobody was ever disturbed. Nobody's feelings were ever hurt. Nobody in all the parish had ever heard a voice of thunder saying, Thou art the man. Toothless and timid generalities made up all the preaching they ever heard either on the ethical or on the evangelical side: and generalities disturb no man's peace of mind. The pulpit of Kilmacolm was but too sib to the pew, and both pulpit and pew slept on together in undisturbed security. And that supplied Samuel Rutherford with an excellent text for a sermon he was continually preaching in every utterance of his--the constant danger we all lie under as long as we are in this life. Danger from sin, and, in its own still subtler way, as much danger from grace; danger from want, and danger from fulness; danger from our weakness, and danger from our strength. So much danger is there that if any man in this life is in a state of security about himself he is surely the foolishest of all foolish men. For,

Thy close pursuers' busy hands do plant
Snares in thy substance, snares attend thy want;
Snares in thy credit, snares in thy disgrace;
Snares in thy high estate, snares in thy base;
Snares tuck thy bed, and snares attend thy board;
Snares watch thy thoughts, and snares attack thy word;
Snares in thy quiet, snares in thy commotion;
Snares in thy diet, snares in thy devotion;
Snares lurk in thy resolves, snares in thy doubt;
Snares lurk within thy heart, and snares without;
Snares are above thy head, and snares beneath;
Snares in thy sickness, snares are in thy death.

What a fool and what a sluggard nature must be, as Rutherford here says she is, if she can lull us into security about ourselves in such a life as this! And what a noble field does this snare-filled life supply for all a preacher's boldest and best powers!

2. They have some new beginners in Kilmacolm in spite of all its spiritual stagnation, and the older people are full of anxiety lest those new beginners should not be rightly directed. 'Tell them for one thing,' says Rutherford in reply, 'to dig deep while they are yet among their foundations. Tell them that a sick night for sin is not so common either among young or old as I would like to see it. Make them to understand what I mean by digging deep. I mean deep into their own heart in order to discover and lay bare to themselves the corrupt motives from which they act every day even in the very best things they do. And that of itself will give them many sufficiently sick days and nights too, both as new beginners and as old believers. And tell them, also, from me, that once they have seen themselves in their own hearts, and Jesus Christ in His heart, it will be impossible for them ever to go back from Him. Absolutely impossible. So much so that it is perfectly certain that he who goes back from Christ has never really seen himself or Christ either. He may have seen something somewhat more or less like Christ, but, all the time, it was not Christ. Let your soul once come up to close quarters with Christ, and I defy you ever to forget Him again. Tell all your new beginners that from me, Samuel

Rutherford, who, after all, am not yet well begun myself.'

3. 'You complain bitterly of a dead ministry in your bounds. I have heard as much. But I will reply that a living ministry is not indispensable to a parish. All our parishes ought to have it, and we ought to see to it that they all get it; but neither the conversion of sinners, nor the sanctification and comfort of God's saints, is tied up to any man's lips. You will read your unread Bibles more: you will buy more good books: you will meet more in private converse and prayer: and it will not be bad for you for a season to look above the pulpit, and to look Jesus Christ Himself more immediately in the face.' As Fraser of Brea also said in a striking passage in his diary, so Rutherford says in his reply letter: 'in your sore famine of the water of life, run your pipe right up to the fountain.'

4. If the parishioners of Kilmacolm were severe on their minister it was not that they let themselves escape. And there was something in their present letters that led Rutherford to warn them against a mistake that only people of the Kilmacolm type will ever fall into. 'Some of the people of God,' says their sharp-eyed censor, 'slander the grace of God in their own soul.' And that is true of some of God's best people still. We meet with such people now and then in our own parishes to-day. They are so possessed with penitence and humility; they have such high and inflexible and spiritual standards for measuring themselves by; the law has so fatally entered their innermost souls that they will not even admit or acknowledge what the grace of God has, to all other men's knowledge, done in them. Seek out, says Rutherford, the signs of true grace in yourselves as well as the signs of secret sin. And when you have found such and such an indubitable sign of grace, say so. Say *this*, and *this*, and *this*, pointing it out, is assuredly the work of God in my soul. When you, after all defeat, really discover your soul growing in grace; in patience under injuries; in meekness under reproofs and corrections; in love for, or at least in peace of heart toward, those you at one time did not like, but disliked almost to downright hatred; in silent and assenting acceptance, if not yet in actual and positive enjoyment, of another man's talents and success, gain and fame; in the decay and disappearance of party spirit, and in openness to all the good and the merit of other men; in prayerfulness; in liberality, and so on; when you cannot deny these things in yourself, then speak good of Christ, and do not traduce and backbite His work because it is in your own soul. 'Some wretches murmur of want while all

the time their money in the bank and their fat harvests make them liars.' Rutherford thinks he has put his finger upon some such saintly liars in the kirk-session of Kilmacolm.

5. 'Fear your light, my lord,' wrote Rutherford to Lord Craighall from Aberdeen; 'stand in awe of your light.' But the poor Kilmacolm people did not need that sharp rebuke, for they had written to Rutherford at their own instance to consult him in their terror of conscience about this very matter, till Rutherford had to exhaust his vocabulary of comfort in trying to pacify his correspondents just in this sufficiently disquieting matter of light in the mind with great darkness in the heart and the life. Our light in this world, he tells them, is a broad and shining field, whereas our life of obedience is at best but a short and straggling furrow. Only in heaven shall the broad and basking fields of light and truth be covered from end to end with the songs of the rejoicing reapers. And Rutherford is very bold in this matter, because he knows he has the truth about it. A perfect life, he says, up to our ever-increasing light, is impossible to us here, if only because our light always increases with every new progress in duty. The field of light expands to a new length and breadth every time the plough passes through it. And, knowing well to whom he writes on this subject, Rutherford goes on to say that there is a sorrow for sin, and for shortcoming in service, that is as acceptable with God in the evangelical covenant as would be the very service itself. But, then, it must be what Rutherford calls 'honest sorrow after a sincere aim.' And let no man easily allow himself to take shelter under that, lest it turn out to him like taking shelter in a thunderstorm under a lightning rod. For what an aim must that be, and then, what a sorrow, that is as good in the sight of God as a full obedience is itself. At the same time, 'A sincere aim, and then an honest sorrow, both of the right quality and quantity, taken together with Christ's intercession, must be our best life before God till we be over in the other country where the law of God will get a perfect soul in which to fulfil itself. Your complaint on this head is already booked in the New Testament (Rom. vii. 18).'

6. 'The less sense of liberty and sweetness, the more true spirituality in the service of God,' is Rutherford's reply to their next perplexity. Ought we to go on with our work and with our worship when our hearts are dry and when we have no delight in what we do? That is just the time to persevere, replies their evangelical guide, for it is in the absence of all sense of liberty and sweetness that our du-

ties prove themselves to be truly spiritual. A sweet service has often its sweetness from an altogether other source than the spiritual world. Let a man be engaged in divine service, or in any other religious work, and let him have sensible support and success in it; let him have liberty and enjoyment in the performance of it; and, especially, let him have the praise of men after it, and he will easily be deceived into thinking that he has had God's Spirit with him, and the light of God's countenance, whereas all the time it has only been an outpouring on his deceived heart of his own lying spirit of self-seeking, self-pleasing, and self-exalting. While, again, a man's spirit may be all day as dry as the heath in the wilderness, and all other men's spirits around him and toward him the same, yet a very rich score may be set down beside that unindulged servant's name against the day of the 'well-dones.' 'I believe that many think that obedience is lifeless and formal unless the wind be in the west, and all their sails are filled with the joys of sense. But I am not of their mind who think so.'

7. The scrupulosity of the Kilmacolm people was surely singular and remarkable even in that day of tests and marks and scruples in the spiritual life. The ministry may not have been wholly dead in and around Kilmacolm, though it could not keep pace and patience with those so eager and so anxious souls who would have Rutherford's mind on all possible points of their complicated case. Six of their complaints we have just seen, but their troubles are not yet all told. 'Surely,' they wrote, 'a Master like our Lord, who gave such service when He was still a servant Himself,--surely He will have hearty and unfeigned service from us, or none at all. Will He not spue the lukewarm servant out of His mouth?' I grant you, wrote Rutherford, that our Master must have honesty. The one thing He will unmask and will not endure is hypocrisy. But if you mean to insinuate that our hearts must always be entirely given up to His service in all that we do, else He will cast us away, for all I am worth in the world I would not have that true of me. I would not have that true, else where would my hope be? An English contemporary of Rutherford's puts it memorably: 'Our Master tries His servants not with the balances of the sanctuary, but with the touchstone.' Take that, says Rutherford, for my reply to your opinion that Christ must always have a perfect service at our hands, or none at all.

8. Again, hold by the ground-work when the outworks and the superstructure are assailed. Fall back the more nakedly upon your sure foundation. Keep the

ground of your standing and acceptance clear, and take your stand on that ground at every time when despair assaults you. For great faults and for small, for formality in spiritual service, for cold-heartedness and for half-heartedness, you have always open to you your old and sure ground, the blood and the righteousness of your Covenant-surety. 'Seek still the blood of atonement for faults much and little. Know the gate to the fountain, and lie about it. Make much of assurance, for it keepeth the anchor fixed.'

9.  The last paragraph of Rutherford's letter to the parishioners of Kilmacolm is taken up with the consolation that always comes to a Christian man's heart after every deed of true self-mortification. That is an experience that all Christian men must often have, whether they take note sufficiently of it or no. Let any man suffer for Christ's sake; let any man be evil-entreated and for Christ's sake take it patiently; let him be reviled and persecuted in public or in private for the truth; let him deny himself some indulgence--allowed, doubtful, or condemned--and all truly for the sake of Christ and other men; and immediately, and as a consequence of that, a peace, a liberty, a light as of God's countenance will infallibly visit his heart. After temptation resisted and overcome angels will always visit us. 'Temptations,' says Bunyan in the fine preface to his **Grace Abounding**, 'when we meet them first are as the lion that roared upon Samson; but, if we overcome them, the next time we see them we shall find a nest of honey within them.' 'Blessed are they that mourn,' says our Lord, 'for they shall be comforted.' 'After my greatest mortifications,' said Edwards, 'I always find my greatest comforts.' And even Renan tells us of a Roman lady who had 'the ineffable joy of renouncing joy.' 'A Christ bought with strokes,' says Rutherford in closing, 'is the sweetest of all Christs.'

### The Codes Of Hammurabi And Moses
### W. W. Davies

QTY

The discovery of the Hammurabi Code is one of the greatest achievements of archaeology, and is of paramount interest, not only to the student of the Bible, but also to all those interested in ancient history...

**Religion**     **ISBN:** *1-59462-338-4*          **Pages:132**
                                                    *MSRP $12.95*

### The Theory of Moral Sentiments
### Adam Smith

QTY

This work from 1749. contains original theories of conscience amd moral judgment and it is the foundation for systemof morals.

**Philosophy**  **ISBN:** *1-59462-777-0*          **Pages:536**
                                                    *MSRP $19.95*

### Jessica's First Prayer
### Hesba Stretton

QTY

In a screened and secluded corner of one of the many railway-bridges which span the streets of London there could be seen a few years ago, from five o'clock every morning until half past eight, a tidily set-out coffee-stall, consisting of a trestle and board, upon which stood two large tin cans, with a small fire of charcoal burning under each so as to keep the coffee boiling during the early hours of the morning when the work-people were thronging into the city on their way to their daily toil...

**Childrens**     **ISBN:** *1-59462-373-2*          **Pages:84**
                                                     *MSRP $9.95*

### My Life and Work
### Henry Ford

QTY

Henry Ford revolutionized the world with his implementation of mass production for the Model T automobile. Gain valuable business insight into his life and work with his own auto-biography... "We have only started on our development of our country we have not as yet, with all our talk of wonderful progress, done more than scratch the surface. The progress has been wonderful enough but..."

**Biographies/**   **ISBN:** *1-59462-198-5*          **Pages:300**
                                                      *MSRP $21.95*

## The Art of Cross-Examination
## Francis Wellman

QTY

I presume it is the experience of every author, after his first book is published upon an important subject, to be almost overwhelmed with a wealth of ideas and illustrations which could readily have been included in his book, and which to his own mind, at least, seem to make a second edition inevitable. Such certainly was the case with me; and when the first edition had reached its sixth impression in five months, I rejoiced to learn that it seemed to my publishers that the book had met with a sufficiently favorable reception to justify a second and considerably enlarged edition. ..

**Pages:412**

Reference     ISBN: *1-59462-647-2*      *MSRP $19.95*

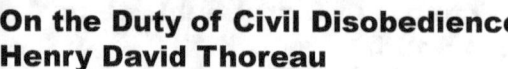

## On the Duty of Civil Disobedience
## Henry David Thoreau

QTY

Thoreau wrote his famous essay, On the Duty of Civil Disobedience, as a protest against an unjust but popular war and the immoral but popular institution of slave-owning. He did more than write—he declined to pay his taxes, and was hauled off to gaol in consequence. Who can say how much this refusal of his hastened the end of the war and of slavery ?

Law         ISBN: *1-59462-747-9*       **Pages:48**

*MSRP $7.45*

## Dream Psychology Psychoanalysis for Beginners
## Sigmund Freud

QTY

Sigmund Freud, born Sigismund Schlomo Freud (May 6, 1856 - September 23, 1939), was a Jewish-Austrian neurologist and psychiatrist who co-founded the psychoanalytic school of psychology. Freud is best known for his theories of the unconscious mind, especially involving the mechanism of repression; his redefinition of sexual desire as mobile and directed towards a wide variety of objects; and his therapeutic techniques, especially his understanding of transference in the therapeutic relationship and the presumed value of dreams as sources of insight into unconscious desires.

**Pages:196**

Psychology    ISBN: *1-59462-905-6*     *MSRP $15.45*

## The Miracle of Right Thought
## Orison Swett Marden

QTY

Believe with all of your heart that you will do what you were made to do. When the mind has once formed the habit of holding cheerful, happy, prosperous pictures, it will not be easy to form the opposite habit. It does not matter how improbable or how far away this realization may see, or how dark the prospects may be, if we visualize them as best we can, as vividly as possible, hold tenaciously to them and vigorously struggle to attain them, they will gradually become actualized, realized in the life. But a desire, a longing without endeavor, a yearning abandoned or held indifferently will vanish without realization.

**Pages:360**

Self Help       ISBN: *1-59462-644-8*      *MSRP $25.45*

QTY

**The Rosicrucian Cosmo-Conception Mystic Christianity** *by Max Heindel*     ISBN: *1-59462-188-8*   **$38.95**
*The Rosicrucian Cosmo-conception is not dogmatic, neither does it appeal to any other authority than the reason of the student. It is: not controversial, but is: sent forth in the, hope that it may help to clear..*     *New Age/Religion Pages 646*

**Abandonment To Divine Providence** *by Jean-Pierre de Caussade*     ISBN: *1-59462-228-0*   **$25.95**
*"The Rev. Jean Pierre de Caussade was one of the most remarkable spiritual writers of the Society of Jesus in France in the 18th Century. His death took place at Toulouse in 1751. His works have gone through many editions and have been republished...*     *Inspirational/Religion Pages 400*

**Mental Chemistry** *by Charles Haanel*     ISBN: *1-59462-192-6*   **$23.95**
*Mental Chemistry allows the change of material conditions by combining and appropriately utilizing the power of the mind. Much like applied chemistry creates something new and unique out of careful combinations of chemicals the mastery of mental chemistry...*     *New Age Pages 354*

**The Letters of Robert Browning and Elizabeth Barret Barrett 1845-1846 vol II**     ISBN: *1-59462-193-4*   **$35.95**
*by Robert Browning and Elizabeth Barrett*     *Biographies Pages 596*

**Gleanings In Genesis (volume I)** *by Arthur W. Pink*     ISBN: *1-59462-130-6*   **$27.45**
*Appropriately has Genesis been termed "the seed plot of the Bible" for in it we have, in germ form, almost all of the great doctrines which are afterwards fully developed in the books of Scripture which follow...*     *Religion/Inspirational Pages 420*

**The Master Key** *by L. W. de Laurence*     ISBN: *1-59462-001-6*   **$30.95**
*In no branch of human knowledge has there been a more lively increase of the spirit of research during the past few years than in the study of Psychology, Concentration and Mental Discipline. The requests for authentic lessons in Thought Control, Mental Discipline and...*     *New Age/Business Pages 422*

**The Lesser Key Of Solomon Goetia** *by L. W. de Laurence*     ISBN: *1-59462-092-X*   **$9.95**
*This translation of the first book of the "Lernegton" which is now for the first time made accessible to students of Talismanic Magic was done, after careful collation and edition, from numerous Ancient Manuscripts in Hebrew, Latin, and French..,*     *New Age/Occult Pages 92*

**Rubaiyat Of Omar Khayyam** *by Edward Fitzgerald*     ISBN:*1-59462-332-5*   **$13.95**
*Edward Fitzgerald, whom the world has already learned, in spite of his own efforts to remain within the shadow of anonymity, to look upon as one of the rarest poets of the century, was born at Bredfield, in Suffolk, on the 31st of March, 1809. He was the third son of John Purcell...*     *Music Pages 172*

**Ancient Law** *by Henry Maine*     ISBN: *1-59462-128-4*   **$29.95**
*The chief object of the following pages is to indicate some of the earliest ideas of mankind, as they are reflected in Ancient Law, and to point out the relation of those ideas to modern thought.*     *Religion/History Pages 452*

**Far-Away Stories** *by William J. Locke*     ISBN: *1-59462-129-2*   **$19.45**
*"Good wine needs no bush, but a collection of mixed vintages does. And this book is just such a collection. Some of the stories I do not want to remain buried for ever in the museum files of dead magazine-numbers an author's not unpardonable vanity..."*     *Fiction Pages 272*

**Life of David Crockett** *by David Crockett*     ISBN: *1-59462-250-7*   **$27.45**
*"Colonel David Crockett was one of the most remarkable men of the times in which he lived. Born in humble life, but gifted with a strong will, an indomitable courage, and unremitting perseverance...*     *Biographies/New Age Pages 424*

**Lip-Reading** *by Edward Nitchie*     ISBN: *1-59462-206-X*   **$25.95**
*Edward B. Nitchie, founder of the New York School for the Hard of Hearing, now the Nitchie School of Lip-Reading, Inc, wrote "LIP-READING Principles and Practice". The development and perfecting of this meritorious work on lip-reading was an undertaking...*     *How-to Pages 400*

**A Handbook of Suggestive Therapeutics, Applied Hypnotism, Psychic Science**     ISBN: *1-59462-214-0*   **$24.95**
*by Henry Munro*     *Health/New Age/Health/Self-help Pages 376*

**A Doll's House: and Two Other Plays** *by Henrik Ibsen*     ISBN: *1-59462-112-8*   **$19.95**
*Henrik Ibsen created this classic when in revolutionary 1848 Rome. Introducing some striking concepts in playwriting for the realist genre, this play has been studied the world over.*     *Fiction/Classics/Plays 308*

**The Light of Asia** *by sir Edwin Arnold*     ISBN: *1-59462-204-3*   **$13.95**
*In this poetic masterpiece, Edwin Arnold describes the life and teachings of Buddha. The man who was to become known as Buddha to the world was born as Prince Gautama of India but he rejected the worldly riches and abandoned the reigns of power when...*     *Religion/History/Biographies Pages 170*

**The Complete Works of Guy de Maupassant** *by Guy de Maupassant*     ISBN: *1-59462-157-8*   **$16.95**
*"For days and days, nights and nights, I had dreamed of that first kiss which was to consecrate our engagement, and I knew not on what spot I should put my lips..."*     *Fiction/Classics Pages 240*

**The Art of Cross-Examination** *by Francis L. Wellman*     ISBN: *1-59462-309-0*   **$26.95**
*Written by a renowned trial lawyer, Wellman imparts his experience and uses case studies to explain how to use psychology to extract desired information through questioning.*     *How-to/Science/Reference Pages 408*

**Answered or Unanswered?** *by Louisa Vaughan*     ISBN: *1-59462-248-5*   **$10.95**
*Miracles of Faith in China*     *Religion Pages 112*

**The Edinburgh Lectures on Mental Science (1909)** *by Thomas*     ISBN: *1-59462-008-3*   **$11.95**
*This book contains the substance of a course of lectures recently given by the writer in the Queen Street Hail, Edinburgh. Its purpose is to indicate the Natural Principles governing the relation between Mental Action and Material Conditions...*     *New Age/Psychology Pages 148*

**Ayesha** *by H. Rider Haggard*     ISBN: *1-59462-301-5*   **$24.95**
*Verily and indeed it is the unexpected that happens! Probably if there was one person upon the earth from whom the Editor of this, and of a certain previous history, did not expect to hear again...*     *Classics Pages 380*

**Ayala's Angel** *by Anthony Trollope*     ISBN: *1-59462-352-X*   **$29.95**
*The two girls were both pretty, but Lucy who was twenty-one who supposed to be simple and comparatively unattractive, whereas Ayala was credited, as her Bombwhat romantic name might show, with poetic charm and a taste for romance. Ayala when her father died was nineteen...*     *Fiction Pages 484*

**The American Commonwealth** *by James Bryce*     ISBN: *1-59462-286-8*   **$34.45**
*An interpretation of American democratic political theory. It examines political mechanics and society from the perspective of Scotsman James Bryce*     *Politics Pages 572*

**Stories of the Pilgrims** *by Margaret P. Pumphrey*     ISBN: *1-59462-116-0*   **$17.95**
*This book explores pilgrims religious oppression in England as well as their escape to Holland and eventual crossing to America on the Mayflower, and their early days in New England...*     *History Pages 268*

QTY

**The Fasting Cure** by *Sinclair Upton*                    ISBN: *1-59462-222-1*  **$13.95**
*In the Cosmopolitan Magazine for May, 1910, and in the Contemporary Review (London) for April, 1910, I published an article dealing with my experiences in fasting. I have written a great many magazine articles, but never one which attracted so much attention...  New Age/Self Help/Health Pages 164*

**Hebrew Astrology** by *Sepharial*                    ISBN: *1-59462-308-2*  **$13.45**
*In these days of advanced thinking it is a matter of common observation that we have left many of the old landmarks behind and that we are now pressing forward to greater heights and to a wider horizon than that which represented the mind-content of our progenitors...  Astrology Pages 144*

**Thought Vibration or The Law of Attraction in the Thought World**    ISBN: *1-59462-127-6*  **$12.95**
by *William Walker Atkinson*                    *Psychology/Religion Pages 144*

**Optimism** by *Helen Keller*                    ISBN: *1-59462-108-X*  **$15.95**
*Helen Keller was blind, deaf, and mute since 19 months old, yet famously learned how to overcome these handicaps, communicate with the world, and spread her lectures promoting optimism. An inspiring read for everyone...  Biographies/Inspirational Pages 84*

**Sara Crewe** by *Frances Burnett*                    ISBN: *1-59462-360-0*  **$9.45**
*In the first place, Miss Minchin lived in London. Her home was a large, dull, tall one, in a large, dull square, where all the houses were alike, and all the sparrows were alike, and where all the door-knockers made the same heavy sound...  Childrens/Classic Pages 88*

**The Autobiography of Benjamin Franklin** by *Benjamin Franklin*    ISBN: *1-59462-135-7*  **$24.95**
*The Autobiography of Benjamin Franklin has probably been more extensively read than any other American historical work, and no other book of its kind has had such ups and downs of fortune. Franklin lived for many years in England, where he was agent...  Biographies/History Pages 332*

| Name | |
|---|---|
| Email | |
| Telephone | |
| Address | |
| | |
| City, State ZIP | |

☐ **Credit Card**          ☐ **Check / Money Order**

| Credit Card Number | |
|---|---|
| Expiration Date | |
| Signature | |

*Please Mail to:*   Book Jungle
                    PO Box 2226
                    Champaign, IL 61825
*or Fax to:*        630-214-0564

www.ingramcontent.com/pod-product-compliance
Lightning Source LLC
Chambersburg PA
CBHW080823020726
47501CB00009B/2395